W9-AYE-476

## THE NOISE OF GUNS BLASTING
## WAS DEAFENING.

A bullet chewed splinters from the door next to Longarm's head, and a couple of the slivers sliced into his cheek and drew his attention back to that side. He opened up with the Winchester. His first shot drove into the chest of one of the outlaws and drove the man backward off his horse like a giant fist.

Longarm jacked the rifle's lever and fired again. He heard the dull boom of Pryor's shotgun and the sharper sound of George's pistol as the two men got into the fight. For a handful of seconds that seemed much longer, guns roared, bullets sang, and the draw was filled with noise and flame and the sharp tang of gun smoke.

Then, with an eerie suddenness like a curtain dropping in a play, the shooting stopped.

## DON'T MISS THESE
## ALL-ACTION WESTERN SERIES
## FROM THE BERKLEY PUBLISHING GROUP

**THE GUNSMITH by J. R. Roberts**
Clint Adams was a legend among lawmen, outlaws, and ladies. They called him . . . the Gunsmith.

**LONGARM by Tabor Evans**
The popular long-running series about U.S. Deputy Marshal Long—his life, his loves, his fight for justice.

**SLOCUM by Jake Logan**
Today's longest-running action Western. John Slocum rides a deadly trail of hot blood and cold steel.

**BUSHWHACKERS by B. J. Lanagan**
An action-packed series by the creators of Longarm! The rousing adventures of the most brutal gang of cutthroats ever assembled—Quantrill's Raiders.

**TABOR EVANS**

# LONGARM

## AND THE RED-LIGHT LADIES

JOVE BOOKS, NEW YORK

If you purchased this book without a cover, you should be aware that this book is stolen property. It was reported as "unsold and destroyed" to the publisher, and neither the author nor the publisher has received any payment for this "stripped book."

LONGARM AND THE RED-LIGHT LADIES

A Jove Book / published by arrangement with
the author

PRINTING HISTORY
Jove edition / February 1999

All rights reserved.
Copyright © 1999 by Jove Publications, Inc.
This book may not be reproduced in whole
or in part, by mimeograph or any other means,
without permission. For information address:
The Berkley Publishing Group, a member of Penguin Putnam Inc.,
375 Hudson Street, New York, New York 10014.

The Penguin Putnam Inc. World Wide Web site address is
http://www.penguinputnam.com

ISBN: 0-515-12450-8

A JOVE BOOK®
Jove Books are published by The Berkley Publishing Group,
a member of Penguin Putnam Inc.,
375 Hudson Street, New York, New York 10014.
JOVE and the "J" design are trademarks belonging to Jove
Publications, Inc.

PRINTED IN THE UNITED STATES OF AMERICA

10  9  8  7  6  5  4  3  2  1

# Chapter 1

The man stumbled along the main street of Galena City, Nevada, muttering to himself as he tried to stay upright. Seeing a drunk in such a condition wasn't anything unusual in these parts. Galena City was a boomtown, after all, having sprung up literally overnight from almost nothing after a rich lode of silver ore was discovered in the nearby mountains. There had been trouble earlier in the evening, but everyone had forgotten about it by now. The saloons that lined both sides of Greenwood Avenue were open twenty-four hours a day, and their business never really slacked off that much. There were always plenty of thirsty miners ready to belly up to the bar.

So no one on the boardwalks of the town paid much attention to the unsteady figure making its way along the muddy street. The man was tall and might have been an impressive physical specimen under other circumstances. He was fairly well dressed, wearing high-topped black boots that were now caked heavily with mud, denim trousers, and a sheepskin coat over a light blue work shirt. His broad-brimmed, flat-crowned, snuff-colored Stetson was pulled down so that it obscured his face. The bottom of a holster poked out from under the left side of his coat, and the way it was turned indicated that it was part of a cross-draw rig.

1

The man careened to the right and then to the left. Galena City's respectable citizens, a few of which were still out and about at this time of the evening, noted the man's staggering progress and clucked their tongues in disapproval. It was bad enough that the town was full of saloons; the least their patrons could do was keep their drunken antics out of sight.

A couple of blocks back up the street, several men came quickly around a corner. They stopped and looked around, their eyes narrow with suspicion and anger. Their hands hovered near the butts of the revolvers holstered on their hips. "Where the hell did he go?" one of them muttered.

"Down there!" another man said abruptly. He lifted his arm and pointed in the direction the tall man had taken.

"Let's get the son of a bitch!"

If the tall man knew he was being pursued, he gave no sign of it. One step after another. Just mastering that concept was enough of a challenge in the shape he was in. It was sheer luck that made him veer crazily toward the boardwalk on the right-hand side of the street. Almost losing his balance, he caught hold of the hitch rack in front of the boardwalk to hold himself up.

His head turned slowly to the side, and his blurry vision suddenly locked on the men hurrying toward him. "Shit!" he said, his voice thick and choked but the exclamation no less heartfelt. He pushed off from the hitch rack and started down the street again, moving a little faster now but still stumbling from side to side.

He couldn't let them catch him out here on the street and drag him into some shadow-laden alley. That would be the end of him. He had to get to someplace where there were plenty of people. Witnesses. His pursuers were less likely to do anything to him if there were a lot of people around to see it.

His numbed muscles would only work so fast, though. The men behind him were rapidly catching up. The tall man gritted his teeth and forced himself to increase his pace. His head swam wildly, and the world seemed to be turning back-

2

ward around him. He felt as if he was running up a steep slope, but he knew that although Galena City was surrounded by mountains, the town itself was built on a flat bench between two peaks. The angle was just a trick of his muddled mind.

Suddenly, one of his boots slipped on a particularly slick stretch of mud, and he fell forward, instinctively thrusting out his hands to catch himself. His clothes were already splattered with mud, and now they were covered with the thick, sticky stuff as he sprawled on the ground. He tried to scramble to his feet again, but his boots kept slipping.

A strong hand closed around his arm, and for a second he thought that they had caught him, that it was all over for him. But then he was lifted, and the face of a stranger peered into his. The man who had come to his aid was tall and beefy. The light that fell into the street from a nearby building revealed rough-hewn features. "Let me give you a hand, my friend," the rescuer said.

"Much . . . much obliged," rasped the tall man, barely able to force the words out through his dry throat. His muddy clothes clung to him uncomfortably, wet and cold.

"You've partaken of too many spirits, my friend," the stranger went on. The tall man noticed now that he wore a black suit and a white collar under a heavier coat. "Let me take you back to the mission—"

"Not . . . not drunk . . ." the tall man managed to get out.

"I know, all you miners think you can hold your liquor. But the demon rum is a tool of the greatest trickster of all, and—"

The tall man glanced painfully over his shoulder and saw that his pursuers had momentarily paused. Clearly, they didn't want to jump him while this sky pilot was haranguing him. The tall man blinked, gave a little shake of his head, winced at the pain of the movement, and said, "Got to go, *padre*. Got to . . . keep movin' . . ."

"What you need is rest and plenty of black coffee," the

3

preacher said sternly. He tugged on the tall man's arm. "Come with me."

It was tempting, but he couldn't do it. There were still things he had to do before he called it a night. Still work to do. He pulled away with surprising strength.

As he did so, his bleary gaze fastened on a building right in front of him, where Greenwood Avenue dead-ended into Comstock Street. It was the largest structure in Galena City, taking up an entire block and standing three stories tall. Gaslights illuminated the long sign emblazoned over the entrance: The Silver Slipper. Even with the doors closed against the cold night air, the sounds of piano music and laughter could be heard coming from inside the saloon.

The tall man started toward the big saloon, drawn toward it for some reason like a moth to a flame. Behind him, the preacher watched him go with a mixture of pity and anger, and a moment later, the men who had been pursuing the tall man brushed roughly past the sky pilot. The preacher sighed. A boomtown such as Galena City was a prime place to do the Lord's work, but sometimes the preacher wondered why he bothered. Most of these sinners were beyond saving.

As he reached the boardwalk in front of the Silver Slipper, the tall man realized he might have set himself up for an insurmountable problem. He didn't think he could manage the steps leading up to the walk. Maybe there was a side door, he thought as he turned shakily to the right.

"Hold it!"

The shout came from less than a block away. No time to waste now. The tall man reached inside himself and drew on the last of his strength. He broke into a shambling run that carried him into the alley beside the Silver Slipper.

Behind him, the sound he had been waiting for—the sound he had been dreading—finally came.

Gunshots rapped out, startlingly loud even in the raucous atmosphere of the boomtown.

The tall man kept moving, expecting at any second to feel a bullet slam into him. The shadows in the alley were thick,

4

however, and although he heard a couple of slugs whine past him too close for comfort, none of them struck him.

A line of light suddenly appeared in the darkness to his left. A door was opening in the side of the saloon building. The tall man threw himself toward it, even as a female voice called out in surprise, "What the hell—!"

His shoulder smacked into the door and threw it open. It hit someone inside, drawing a startled yelp of pain. The tall man reached out blindly, dazzled by the lamplight inside the room, and found the edge of the door. He slammed it shut behind him.

"Lock it! Bar it! Something!" he said hoarsely. His feet got tangled in a throw rug on the floor, and he struggled to maintain his balance. Vaguely, he heard a wooden bar dropping into prongs on each side of the door, barring the entrance. He saw a desk littered with papers. The light came from a lamp on the desk. Dizzily, he reached for the desk, intending to use it to hold himself up, but his hand slipped and he fell. Fortunately, there was a divan against the wall near the desk, and he sprawled on it instead of the floor. His hat fell off, revealing a thatch of dark brown hair, a lean face, and a longhorn mustache. He looked up at the room's other occupant.

She was a redheaded woman around thirty, and a part of the man's brain that was still working told him that she was quite lovely. She wore a dark green gown, cut low to reveal the creamy swells of her breasts.

And she had a small pistol in her hand, pointed directly at him. Her eyes flashed angrily as she stared at him and demanded, "Just who the hell do you think you are, mister? You come in here drunk as a skunk and knock me around and fall on my divan and get mud all over it—" She stopped short, gasping as his coat fell open and revealed a large stain on his shirt that wasn't mud. After swallowing hard, she went on. "My God, is that blood?"

"Sorry for the . . . mess," the man said. "I'll try not to . . . die on you . . ."

5

Then his head fell back and he started sliding away down a long slope with nothing but blackness at the bottom of it. He felt the woman's hands on him, but he couldn't stop his headlong plunge and neither could she. But before the blackness swallowed him, he heard her say in surprise, "Good Lord! He's a U.S. marshal . . ."

# Chapter 2

"Warm for this time of year, ain't it?" Chief Marshal Billy Vail had said in his Denver office a week earlier.

*Uh-oh*, thought Longarm as he leaned back in the red leather chair in front of Vail's desk and propped his right ankle on his left knee. Billy was talking about the weather. That couldn't be a good sign. The pudgy chief marshal wasn't much on small talk. If he was avoiding the real reason he had summoned Longarm here this morning, there had to be a good excuse for it.

Like maybe the job Billy was about to hand to him was a real bitch.

Longarm slid a cheroot from his vest pocket, bit off the end, dug out a lucifer, and set fire to the smoke. He shook out the match and dropped it on the floor beside the chair, which would drive poor Henry crazy. Vail's assistant liked things all neat and tidy.

"It's warm, all right," Longarm said warily around the cheroot.

"Still pretty cold up in the high country, though, I'd wager."

Longarm nodded slowly. "More than likely." He didn't point out that although Denver was situated on the plains, it was pretty high itself. Just about a mile in elevation, in fact.

"Got a job for you over in Nevada," Vail said as he looked down at the papers on his desk. "A gang of owlhoots over there has been stopping and robbing stagecoaches in the silver-mining country."

"They must've heisted a mailbag or two," said Longarm, "else the local law wouldn't be calling in Uncle Sam."

"That's right. Only they weren't after the mail itself. Some of those mine owners got the bright idea that they could ship out their ore by putting it in the bottom of a mail sack and then covering it up with the regular mail."

Longarm winced. "That might've worked a time or two, but it'd be hell keeping something like that a secret. Too many people would have to know about it."

"That's right," Vail agreed. "But it hasn't stopped the mine owners. They're stubborn, and they insist it's no different from mailing anything else. It's the responsibility of the federal government to keep the mail safe."

"And in this case, the federal government is represented by yours truly."

Vail nodded. "That's right. Henry's got your travel vouchers in the other office. You can take the train from here to Salt Lake and then on over to Carson City. From there you'll have to go on horseback, though. All the robberies have been on the stage line that runs from Virginia City on down through Carson City to Rawhide and Tonopah and Galena City."

"You think one gang's responsible for all the robberies?" asked Longarm.

"That's what it looks like so far. All the holdups have been similar, and the holdup men have been dressed alike each time. It's one bunch, all right."

"I'm supposed to run 'em to ground, bring 'em in, and recover all the loot they've stolen so far?"

"That's the idea," Vail said dryly. "Think you can handle it?"

Longarm frowned slightly. He couldn't understand why Billy had been ducking the issue earlier. This looked like a simple assignment, no different from dozens of others he had carried out in the past. He said bluntly, "There's something you're not telling me, Billy."

"Well, there *is* the matter of the killings," Vail admitted. "During each robbery, they've gunned down at least one person. No reason, mind you. All the victims tried to cooperate."

"Oh, there was a reason, all right," muttered Longarm. He leaned forward and stubbed out the butt of his cheroot in the ashtray on Vail's desk.

"What's that?"

"Sounds to me like they just plain enjoy killing folks," Longarm said.

Longarm leaned back against his seat in the railroad car and stretched out his legs as best he could in the cramped space. The left one extended into the aisle. It was difficult for someone as tall as Longarm to sit comfortably in these seats, especially for long periods of time, such as the journey from Denver to Carson City. Thankfully, the train would be pulling into the Nevada capital in another hour or so. Longarm wouldn't have to endure the discomfort any longer than that.

It would have been better if the Justice Department was willing to spring for a sleeper compartment instead of just a seat in a day coach, but Longarm knew better than to expect that. The government could always find what they considered better things to spend their money on.

He fished out a cheroot and had lit it and taken a big puff before he became aware that he was being frowned at in disapproval by a woman sitting across the aisle. She had boarded the train at Salt Lake City, and Longarm had taken note of her then, as he usually did whenever he saw a woman who was young and pretty and not sporting a wedding ring on her finger. This one was wearing a somber dark brown dress and hat, but the outfit couldn't completely disguise her beauty. The hair under the hat was soft and blond, and the body under the brown dress was slender yet more than adequately curved. Her eyes were probably brown, Longarm thought, but he wasn't sure because her gaze had flicked in his direction only once, and very quickly then. She seemed to be careful not to look at the other passengers, especially the men. Her eyes had been kept turned forward for the entire trip, never straying toward the seat on the other side of the aisle where Longarm sat.

So now, as she glared at him, he got his first good look at her eyes, and they were brown just as he had suspected. Not quite as dark a shade as her dress and hat, however. Her eyes had a certain softness to them, too, like her hair.

"Must you smoke that foul thing in here?" she demanded. Longarm held up the cheroot. "This?"

"What else would you be smoking, sir?"

"Sorry if it offends you, ma'am," said Longarm with a shrug. He glanced around the car. "Other folks are smoking in here, so I didn't figure you'd mind." In truth, he hadn't actually given the matter a thought before he lit up.

"Those other folks, as you call them, are not sitting directly across from me so that the noxious smoke from their pipes and cigars wafts directly into my face."

*Wafts?* thought Longarm. He spent a couple of seconds trying to remember when he had last heard someone actually use that word, then gave it up as a bad job. He said, "I reckon if it would make you feel better, ma'am, I could step out on the platform to finish this."

"I wish you would," the young woman said. She sniffed and folded her arms across her chest, then looked away from him again.

Longarm stuck the cheroot back in his mouth, clamped his teeth on it, shook his head, and stood up. He knew his three-for-a-nickel cheroots weren't the best-smelling things in the world, but he wasn't accustomed to being booted out of a railroad car because of them, either.

But, he told himself, anything to please a lady. He stepped out into the aisle and turned toward the door at the rear of the car.

To his surprise, the young woman stood up as well and followed him. When he glanced back at her with a frown, she said, "I intend to see to it that you actually take that thing outside. You might attempt to deceive me by staying there in the rear of the car, where I'm certain the foul odor would still be detectable."

Of all the prissy little bitches . . . ! Longarm controlled his temper with an effort and said, "I told you I'd step out onto the platform, ma'am. I assure you I'm a man of my word."

"I'll determine that for myself, thank you."

Longarm rolled his eyes and walked to the rear of the car, not bothering to look back and see if the woman was still following him. When he reached the door, he jerked it open and stepped out onto the platform. Sure enough, the woman was right behind him.

But instead of closing the door between them, she moved out onto the platform, too, and then shut the door. When Longarm turned and saw her standing there with him, his frown deepened and he took the cheroot out of his mouth to say, "What the hell?"

"Throw that cigar away," the young woman snapped.

Longarm finally gave in to his temper. "I'll be damned if I will!" he said. "I came out here the way you wanted, lady, and if that's not good enough for you—"

"Oh, hush," the woman said, and she stepped forward and came up on her toes to put her arms around his neck and press her mouth to his.

Longarm dropped the cheroot on the platform and put it out blindly with his boot heel as he slid his arms around the woman and returned the kiss. Her lips parted and her tongue darted out brazenly to spear into his mouth. Her breasts flattened under the somber dress as she pressed them against his broad, hard-muscled chest.

When she finally pulled away slightly with a self-satisfied smile on her lovely face, Longarm said, "I was under the impression that you didn't much like me, ma'am. Or maybe

11

it was just my cheroot. If I'd known how grateful you'd be, I'd have put it out a lot sooner.''

"Oh, I don't care about that silly thing one way or the other," she said. "I just wanted to get you out here where we could have some privacy so I could do that. I've been wanting to kiss you ever since I got on the train."

"You did a pretty good job of making sure nobody knew you felt like that," commented Longarm, remembering her chilly demeanor during the trip.

She laughed lightly. "I was just waiting for the right moment." She looked around and added, "Isn't this romantic?"

Longarm supposed it was. The scenery rolling by was pretty, with lots of snow-capped mountains and green pine-covered slopes and brooks laughing and gurgling through deep valleys. But the air blowing around them was cold, and it carried occasional cinders from the locomotive's smokestack that had to be watched out for.

"It's pretty nice," Longarm told the woman. "I reckon you'd make just about any picture prettier, though."

"What a sweet thing to say! My name is Amelia Loftus, by the way."

"Custis Long." He didn't mention the fact that he was a deputy United States marshal. Amelia Loftus didn't have any reason to need to know that.

"I'm very pleased to meet you, Mr. Long." And she kissed him again to prove it.

The second time was just as pleasant as the first, but a worry was beginning to nag at the back of Longarm's mind. He was the one who broke the kiss this time, and when he did, he said, "I'm wondering about something, Miss Loftus. Or is it missus?"

"Oh, it's miss, I assure you. I'm not a married woman, though my father would have had it otherwise. He wanted to make a match for me with one of the elders."

"You're one of the Saints, then." Longarm had figured her for a Mormon, given her clothes and her attitude and the fact that she had boarded the train in Salt Lake City.

"That's right. I have some distinct doctrinal differences with the church, however."

She sure liked to talk fancy, thought Longarm. That made her a poor candidate for being a Mormon right there. They were plain-spoken folks. "What sort of differences?" he asked.

"Well, for one thing, this business of having more than one wife."

"A lot of Mormons are giving that up, or so I've heard tell."

"And well they should. A man has no business having more than one wife." Her lips curved wickedly in a smile. "It would be so much more fun for a woman to have more than one husband, to my way of thinking. Just think about it, Mr. Long. A lady could be pleasured for hours on end! When one husband had exhausted himself, another could simply take his place."

Longarm's eyebrows lifted in surprise. "I reckon that's one way of looking at it," he said.

Amelia Loftus reached down and caressed his groin through his trousers. Her fingers closed around the rapidly growing length of his shaft and she smiled. "Of course, I daresay a man such as yourself might be able to give a lady all the pleasure she could handle all by yourself, Mr. Long."

She was just about the most unusual Mormon woman he had ever met, he thought. But he liked what she was doing to him, and as he leaned toward her, he murmured, "A gentleman always tries to oblige a lady."

Her mouth was wet and hot and sweet. She whispered, "I'll be staying in the Oriental Hotel in Carson City."

"I've got a hunch I will be, too," said Longarm.

# Chapter 3

Amelia rested her hands on Longarm's chest, threw her head back, closed her eyes, and panted, "Oh, yes, Custis! Yes!"

Longarm held on to her slender hips and drove himself deeper into her. Just when he thought his manhood was embedded in her as far as it would go, she pumped her hips to match his thrust and he plumbed new depths. He could feel his climax building, getting ready to boil up through his shaft.

She caught hold of his wrists and brought his hands to her firm, pear-shaped breasts. Her hard nipples stabbed into his palms like little daggers of flesh. Shudders of culmination rippled through her body as Longarm began to empty himself into her in a long series of white-hot spurts. She was still pumping her hips and spasming when he had finished coming. Then, abruptly, she froze in place for a moment, eyes squeezed shut, mouth open, face taut with the ecstasy that gripped her. Her breath came out of her body in a long sigh, and she was suddenly limp, sprawling forward over his chest. She nestled her head against his shoulder and lay there, breathing hard.

Longarm rested one hand on the enticing swell of her bottom and used the other to stroke her hair. He chuckled. "I reckon that's why some folks call it the little death," he said.

"It's damn near as good as dying and going to heaven, ain't it?"

"Don't . . . swear," said Amelia.

"I won't smoke no cheroots, neither, if you don't want me to. But one would taste mighty good right about now."

"In a minute," she said. She patted his chest and snuggled against the thick mat of brown hair. "Just lie there and let me enjoy the feel of you."

Longarm trailed a finger through the cleft between the cheeks of her rump, and his intimate touch made her wiggle her hips. He was still buried inside her, and her movement made his shaft start to stiffen again in response. She lifted her head and her eyes widened in surprise as she exclaimed, "Already?"

Longarm moved his hips. Amelia sighed again, a soft, breathy sound. "Oh, my, yes."

They had managed to keep their hands off each other during dinner, which they had shared in the dining room of Carson City's elegant Oriental Hotel. The bill for Longarm's lodgings here was going to be more expensive than Henry liked, but Longarm figured he could get the clerk to approve it. Henry could be a reasonable man—when he wanted to be.

After dinner, they had come here to Longarm's room for brandy, and the genteel atmosphere that went with the whole situation had lasted for a while.

Almost a whole minute, in fact.

And then they had been pulling each other's clothes off as fast as they could, laughing and stroking and squeezing, until Amelia had pushed Longarm down on the bed, straddled his hips, and lowered herself onto him so that she was riding the long, thick pole of male flesh.

It had been one hell of a ride, and Amelia, bless her heart, was ready to go again.


"I think I'll go to Virginia City," Amelia said. She pinned her hair in place and settled the prim little hat on her head.

15

She was fully dressed and looked every bit the lady again.

Longarm, on the other hand, was still sprawled naked on the bed, his head propped up on the pillows and his hands locked together behind his neck. The air in the room was a little chilly, but he didn't mind. Amelia looked at him in the mirror over the dressing table and said, "You look positively decadent, Custis."

"Thanks," he said with a grin. Then he became more serious as he asked, "You know anybody in Virginia City?"

Amelia turned away from the mirror and shook her head. "No, not a soul," she replied. "Why do you ask?"

Longarm frowned. "To be honest, I'm a mite worried about you. Virginia City's a rough place. It's full of miners and cowboys and gamblers and gunmen."

"It sounds exciting," Amelia said with a smile.

"It ain't the kind of place for a sweet little Mormon gal who don't know what she's getting into," said Longarm bluntly.

Amelia clapped her hands together in delight. "Why, Custis, you're worried about me!"

"Well, of course I'm worried about you. You and me are friends, ain't we?"

"More than friends, I'd say." Amelia's eyebrows lifted and her smile became suggestive.

Longarm sat up and reached for his long underwear. He didn't want Amelia getting any ideas about taking her clothes off again and distracting him from what he wanted to say.

"Listen," he told her, "I know you didn't like living in Utah. I reckon you probably come from a big family—"

"Eight sisters and seven brothers," she said.

"How many wives does your father have?"

"Three. My mother is the oldest."

"And I know you don't have your heart set on living the same way—"

"Elder Torrance has been looking at me ever since I turned fourteen," Amelia broke in, her expression serious now. "That was five years ago, Custis. I'm surprised he's

16

waited this long to start pressuring my father to arrange the marriage."

"How old is this Elder Torrance?"

"Fifty-two. I would be his fifth wife."

"I don't reckon I blame you for not being too fond of the idea. You sound like an educated woman . . ."

"I've read a great deal. My father never wanted my mother to teach me how to read, but she got her own way occasionally. That was one of the occasions. And Father has regretted it ever since."

Longarm pulled his pants on over the long underwear and reached for his shirt. "And you figure you've got a pretty good idea what the rest of the world is like," he went on. "But you don't, Amelia, not really. There are plenty of folks in places like Virginia City who'd take advantage of you."

She glanced at the bed. "Like you did here, Custis?"

His face flushed in a mixture of anger and embarrassment. "This wasn't the first time you'd been with a man," he said.

She shook her head. "No, it wasn't."

"But that doesn't make you the kind of woman that half the men in Virginia City will assume you are. You'd be better off staying here. Living in Carson City ain't like being in church, but it's not as wild and woolly as Virginia City."

"No, and I'd wager it's not as exciting, either." Amelia shook her head. "I'm afraid I've made up my mind, Custis. I want some excitement in my life, and Virginia City is the place where I'll find it."

He sighed heavily. "Then I reckon I'll just have to go up there with you so I can be sure you make it all right."

Her expression was transformed by the smile that spread across it. She threw her arms around his neck and said, "Thank you, Custis, thank you so much."

Longarm patted her on the back and wondered if this was what she had had in mind all along.

He was up early the next morning. Amelia had given him the key to her room, so he unlocked the door quietly and

17

peeked inside. She was still asleep, her breathing soft and regular. Longarm left her there, mounded under the blankets, to sleep in peace.

After breakfast in the hotel dining room, he walked down the street to a building he had spotted the day before on the way from the depot to the hotel. It was a big, barnlike structure, and a sign hanging over the large double doors read California & Nevada Stagecoach Company. A smaller sign below read Burton Augustus Thompson, Esq., Prop. To one side of the double doors was a smaller door, no doubt leading to the offices of the stage line. Longarm went to it and opened it.

A man was sitting at a desk inside the room, which was evidently the office that Longarm had assumed it to be. He wore a gray tweed suit that went well with his longish hair, which was brushed straight back. His cheeks bristled with a short but bushy beard that was mostly gray but had some strands of silver mixed in with the rest. He looked up at Longarm with dark, intelligent eyes.

"Mornin'," the man said with a nod. "What can I do for you, mister?"

"Looking for the ticket agent," said Longarm. "I need to buy a couple of seats on the next stage to Virginia City." He could start his investigation there as well as anywhere. The gang that had been holding up stagecoaches and stealing silver from the mail pouches operated throughout the area.

"I can sell you those tickets," the man said. He stood and extended a hand over the desk. "I'm Thompson, the fella who runs this line. Call me Bat, after my initials."

Longarm grinned. "Like that fella who's the marshal over at Dodge City, eh? I've run into him a time or two."

Bat Thompson winced. "Just once, I hope somebody comes up to Masterson and says his name is like mine. But I reckon if it ever happens, I'll never know about it." He opened a drawer in the desk. "Goin' to Virginny City, are you?"

"That's the plan," said Longarm. Since he had been lucky

enough to encounter the owner of the stage line that had been having so much trouble with outlaws, he decided to do a little probing. He wouldn't reveal to Thompson that he was a deputy marshal, though, not just yet anyway. Longarm had found over the years that he sometimes got better results if he kept his true profession a secret, at least in the early stages of an investigation. He continued, "I hear you've had a little trouble in these parts lately. Holdups and such."

Thompson had taken two tickets from the desk. He surprised Longarm by throwing them onto the floor and jumping up and down on them. Longarm watched in amazement as Thompson continued to jump on the tickets and generally turned the air around his head blue with profanity.

". . . with a red-hot poker, the no-good, lowdown sons o' bitches!" concluded Thompson. "That'd teach 'em!"

"You're talking about the gang that's been stopping your stages?" asked Longarm.

"Who else?" Thompson practically howled. "They're about to run me outta business! The bastards got the federal gov'ment down on me by stealin' silver shipments outta the mailbags!"

Thompson wasn't telling Longarm anything he didn't already know, but Longarm pretended sympathy as he shook his head. "That's too bad. Reckon it's safe to ride your stage?"

That provoked another outburst of profanity from Thompson. He bent over, snatched up the tickets from the floor, and tore them into tiny pieces which he threw into the air. They settled back down around him like snow. "There!" he ranted at Longarm. "If you think you won't be safe, you don't have to ride the damned stage!"

Longarm held up both hands, palms out. "Take it easy, old-timer," he said. "I didn't mean no offense. I just like to know what I'm getting into."

Abruptly, a crestfallen look came over Thompson's face. "Reckon I did it again, didn't I?"

"Did what again?" asked Longarm.

19

"Went plumb crazy. I been doin' that every now and then ever since them holdups started." Thompson brushed aside the pieces of the torn-up tickets that had landed on the desk. "I'm sure sorry, mister. I'll write you up some new tickets. It's just that, well, I built this stage line up from nothin'. Startin' out, I drove the teams and rode shotgun and mucked out the barns. I've put damn near thirty years into it. And now it looks like I'm liable to lose the whole thing, all because o' that damned Mallory!"

"Mallory?" repeated Longarm. He didn't have to pretend to be interested. This might be his first lead.

Bat Thompson nodded. "Fella's name is Ben Mallory. Rumor has it he's the leader o' the gang that's been robbin' me blind."

Longarm shook his head and said, "Never heard of him."

Thompson took two more tickets from the desk drawer and started scrawling on them with a quill pen. "No reason you would have, if you ain't from these parts. He used to be a silver miner before he got fired for causin' too much trouble. And considerin' how rough that crowd is, that'll tell you just what a hellion Mallory is. He swore he'd get even with all the mine superintendents when none of 'em would give him a job, and he started gatherin' up a bunch of other hell-raisers. They rode off into the mountains, and that was the last anybody seen of 'em. But my gut tells me that it's Mallory's bunch who've been hittin' my coaches."

"This fella have a particular grudge against you?"

Thompson shook his head as he handed Longarm the tickets. "Nope. All he wants is the silver. He's got all the superintendents pullin' their hair out and tryin' to figure a way to get their shipments out safe. Mallory hit their ore wagons, and now he's hittin' my coaches 'cause that's where the silver is."

Longarm rasped a thumbnail along the line of his jaw and said, "If I was you, I might tell those mine superintendents they couldn't ship their silver with me anymore."

Thompson sighed wearily. "I've thought about it, believe

me," he said. "But they're just about the most important fellas around here. I have to try to cooperate with 'em if I want to stay in business. It wouldn't pay to cross 'em."

It sounded to Longarm like Thompson was caught between a rock and a hard place, all right.

"Otherwise," Thompson went on, "I wouldn't have agreed to let 'em try to ship another load up here from Tonopah tomorrow."

Longarm perked up even more. "You say there's silver coming up from Tonopah?"

Suddenly, Thompson's face darkened with suspicion. "Say," he exclaimed, "you been askin' a hell of a lot o' questions, mister! Maybe you're a damned spy for Mallory!" His hand dipped toward the still-open drawer of the desk. Longarm knew there was probably a pistol hidden in there.

Sure enough, Thompson hefted an old Dragoon Colt with a barrel that looked as big around as that of a cannon. Longarm stood still and kept his hands in plain sight as Thompson pointed the gun at him. He didn't want to do anything to spook the old man, who had already demonstrated that he could fly off the handle easily.

"I ought to blow your damned head off," grated Thompson.

"That would be a mistake," said Longarm. He kept a tight rein on his instincts. He didn't care for having a gun pointed at him. "I'm not an outlaw, and I never heard of Ben Mallory until you mentioned him. But I've got a good reason for all the questions I'm asking."

"And just what would that be?"

"I'm a deputy U.S. marshal out of Denver. Name's Custis Long. If you'll let me reach in my pocket, I'll show you my badge and bona fides."

Thompson frowned in a mixture of surprise and disbelief. "A lawman, you say?"

"That's right."

Thompson poked the barrel of the massive revolver at

Longarm and said, "Let's see that badge. Take it out slow and easy like."

Longarm reached inside his brown tweed coat and brought out the leather folder that had his badge pinned inside it. The folder contained his identification papers as well. He held it out to Thompson, and when the older man reached for it, Longarm resisted the temptation to slap the gun aside and take it away from him. Thompson glanced back and forth between Longarm and the badge and grunted, "Looks real, all right."

"It is real," Longarm told him. "You can wire my boss, Chief Marshal Billy Vail, if you want any more confirmation of who I really am."

Thompson tossed the folder back to Longarm. "Don't reckon that'll be necessary." He lowered the pistol and put it back in the desk drawer. "Why didn't you tell me right off who you are, instead of askin' a bunch of questions?"

"Sometimes I get better answers when people don't know I work for Uncle Sam." Longarm put away his identification and went on. "What time is that shipment of silver leaving Tonopah tomorrow?"

"Seven in the mornin'."

"Can I get there today?"

"Yeah, but I thought you was goin' to Virginny City," said Thompson.

"So did I," said Longarm.

He just hoped Amelia would be understanding about the change in plans.

# Chapter 4

"I am going to Virginia City, and that's final," said Amelia.

"But I've got to go to Tonopah—"

"With you or without you, Custis, I am going to Virginia City."

Longarm bit back a curse. If the Good Lord had ever put more stubborn creatures than women on the earth, Longarm had never run across them. He made one last attempt to reason with Amelia, saying, "You could stay here in Carson City for a day or two—"

She shook her head and put out her hand. "Give me my ticket. I know you bought them. I'll pay you for it and be on my way."

He had been talking himself blue in the face for half an hour, ever since he had returned to the hotel from Bat Thompson's office and found Amelia awake and dressed and ready to leave. She had even gone downstairs for breakfast while he was talking to the stage line owner.

"I told you, something's come up. But I'll be back in just a couple of days."

"You can come on to Virginia City then and find me if you're concerned about my welfare. I'm certain the place isn't so large that a man of your talents couldn't locate me."

She didn't know anything about his talents, other than the

ones that had pleasured her so much. She didn't even know he was a lawman. He wondered if it would do any good to order her to stay here in Carson City, otherwise he would arrest her.

But on what charge? Longarm figured he could trump something up and get the local badge-toters to go along with it, but would that be the right thing to do? Amelia would hate him if he did that.

He sighed, halfway wishing he had never lit that cheroot on the train and given her an excuse to get to know him. Things would be a lot simpler now if she was just a good-looking stranger who had come and gone without ever speaking to him.

But that wasn't the way things were, and he couldn't change the past. All he could do was take the ticket out of his pocket and slap it into her outstretched hand. The ticket in his other coat pocket was his, and it was for the stagecoach that would be leaving Carson City in less than half an hour bound for Tonopah.

"There," said Longarm. "Good luck to you."

Amelia tried a tentative smile. "You sound like you're not sure you mean that, Custis."

"Oh, I mean it, all right. I wouldn't wish you ill fortune, Amelia. But you're just about the orneriest female I've run across in a while."

Her smile widened. "I'll take that as a compliment. Determination is a good quality in a woman." She came up on her toes and brushed her lips across his. "Goodbye, Custis," she murmured. "Come to see me in Virginia City."

Longarm pulled her into his arms and kissed her hard, leaving her breathless. "I'll be there," he said. "That's a promise."

Longarm stowed his saddle and his warbag in the stage-coach's boot and carried his Winchester as he stepped up to the coach's door. The driver, a stocky, middle-aged man,

24

frowned at him from the box and asked, "You plan on keepin' that rifle with you, mister?"

Bat Thompson came out of the office in time to hear the jehu's question. "It's all right, George," he said. "Mr. Long can keep his Winchester in the coach with him."

George looked from Thompson to Longarm and back again, then nodded curtly. "Sure. If that's what you want, Bat, it's fine with me."

Longarm had asked Thompson to keep quiet about the fact that he was a deputy marshal. George probably figured that Longarm was a special guard Thompson had hired. That was certainly possible, considering all the trouble the stage line had experienced recently.

The coach rocked slightly on its broad leather thoroughbraces as Longarm stepped up into it. There were three other passengers: two men in derby hats and suits whose clothing, red noses, and sample cases proclaimed them to be salesmen of some sort, and a man in rough work clothes, probably a miner, who sat with his battered old hat tipped down over his eyes. He was already snoring loudly. The smell of rotgut whiskey came from him.

The two drummers were sitting next to each other, so Longarm settled himself beside the sleeping man. The drummers looked at Longarm's rifle as he set it on the floor at his feet, but they didn't say anything. Longarm fished a cheroot out of his vest pocket as he glanced over at the man beside him. Chances were, the man was exactly what he appeared to be—a miner who had come to Carson City and gone on a bender. But Longarm knew that acting like a drunk could sometimes be a good disguise. He had used that ploy a time or two himself.

Still, he wasn't expecting any problems on the way from Carson City to Tonopah. If there was going to be trouble, it would likely occur on the return trip, when the stagecoach was carrying a shipment of silver.

A few minutes later, a young man in a long duster, carrying a shotgun and a canvas pouch, came out of the office.

Longarm watched him as he handed the pouch up to the driver, then climbed onto the box. Thompson had told him that the shotgun guard on this trip would be a young fella named Pryor. Despite Pryor's youth, Thompson insisted he was cool-headed and knew how to handle a greener.

George whipped up the team and the coach lurched into motion. Bat Thompson was standing in front of the office, and he lifted a hand in farewell as the coach rolled past. Thompson's face was set in grim lines. He was a man who had seen so much trouble that he was surprised when nothing went wrong, thought Longarm.

The route the stage was following ran southeast out of Carson City, skirting the Wassuk Range and the Excelsior Mountains and hugging the foothills of those peaks. That meant when Longarm looked out the coach's right-hand window, he saw piney slopes and towering, snow-crested mountains, and when he looked the other way, to the left, all that met the eye was the flat brown barrenness of the Great Basin. He sighed, remembering a hellish assignment that had taken him along the Humboldt River through the Great Basin. Of course, given his profession, he could summon up a lot of memories, both good and bad, about most places west of the Mississippi and few places east of the Father of Waters.

The stage had gone several miles when one of the drummers cleared his throat and asked Longarm, "Are you traveling on business, friend?"

"You could say that," Longarm replied as a bump in the road jolted the passengers and made the sleeping man sway over against his shoulder. He shoved the man back into the other corner, and the gent never stopped snoring.

"My name is Avery," the drummer went on. "I sell the finest line of medicinal spirits available anywhere in Nevada."

Longarm nodded but crossed his arms and lied, "I'm afraid I don't indulge, friend, nor have much truck with those who do." He was in no mood to listen to a sales pitch. He

26

was thinking about Amelia and hoping that everything would go all right for her in Virginia City.

With a frown that was almost a pout, Avery leaned back and didn't say anything else. The other drummer grinned broadly at the way Longarm had shut him up.

Around the middle of the day, the stagecoach reached Rawhide and stopped briefly to change teams, but no more passengers boarded. Longarm and his companions ate a quick meal of beans and cornbread and black coffee at the stage station, and then the coach rolled on.

"What time do we get to Tonopah?" asked Longarm.

The miner, who had woken up long enough to drink two cups of coffee but had passed on the food, was already drowsing again. The other drummer said, "We should be there by four."

Longarm took his watch out and flipped it open. The watch was attached to a gold chain that looped across Longarm's chest, and welded to the other end of the chain to serve as a fob was a .44-caliber derringer that had saved Longarm's bacon many times as a hideout gun. He checked the time, snapped the watch closed, put it away. As he leaned back and tipped his hat down over his eyes, he said, "That'll give me the chance for a nice long nap." He hoped Avery and the other drummer would take the hint and leave him alone.

They did, and Longarm dozed off. It was chilly in the coach and the ride was rough, but that didn't keep him from sleeping. Like most men who lived lives of danger, he had perfected the art of getting his rest whenever and wherever he could.

The stage arrived in Tonopah on schedule. Longarm stepped off the coach first, followed by the two drummers and finally the miner. He stumbled away, muttering to himself, and the drummers headed for the town's only hotel, carrying their sample cases. Longarm never had found out what the second drummer sold, and that was fine with him. He stepped into the station's office, which was little more than a lean-to shed built on the side of the barn where the

27

teams were kept. A bald man with bushy side whiskers sat behind a small table made out of scarred planks. He looked up as Longarm came in.

"Are you the stationmaster?" asked Longarm.

The man nodded. "Name's Willard. Can I help you?"

Longarm took a piece of paper from inside his coat. Bat Thompson had scribbled a message on it, folded it, and sealed it with wax. "Your boss told me to give this to you when I got here," said Longarm.

Willard took the message, broke the seal, opened it and read it. When he looked up at Longarm again, there was new respect in his eyes. "Deputy marshal, huh? Reckon I know why you're here. We've got a shipment of silver goin' out tomorrow."

Longarm nodded and said, "Who knows about that besides you and Thompson and the mine superintendents?"

"Nobody," Willard said firmly. "We've kept it quiet as can be. Angus Jenkins—he's the superintendent of the Nevada Belle mine—is bringing the ore into town tonight. The mines have pooled their ore for shipment, and we'll split it up among several mailbags."

"You have that much mail going out from here?" asked Longarm. "Won't it look suspicious to have more than one bag?"

"There are mines scattered all over these hills and mountains, Marshal. Lots of men working up there. Most of 'em have families they write to."

Longarm shrugged and said, "All right, I'll take your word for it. What about the superintendents themselves? You reckon they can be trusted?"

"The fellas who own those mines wouldn't have hired them otherwise," said Willard.

Longarm knew that. He was just trying to think of every possible angle. Someone had to have tipped off this Ben Mallory and his gang about the first shipments of silver hidden in mailbags, but since then the outlaws could have been striking at random, hoping to find more in the pouches than letters.

"What about this fella Mallory?" he asked. "Do you know him?"

"I know him when I see him," replied Willard. "He was always a no-good troublemaker, busted up the saloons here more than once, never could hold a job more than a few weeks."

"I'm told it's probably his gang that's been holding up the stages. You think that's right?"

"I'd say it's damned near certain. Mallory swore he'd make life miserable for everybody in this corner of Nevada, and he's gone a long way toward doing just that. Besides, all that killing . . ." Willard shook his bald head. "That's just like Mallory. You could look in his eyes and see that he had a taste for killing." The stationmaster flattened his palms on the table and took a deep breath. "I tell you, Marshal, I've seen some bad men in my time, but Ben Mallory was one of the worst. Looking at him was like looking at a diamondback rattler."

"How many people have been killed?" asked Longarm.

"Almost a dozen. Five of 'em were guards on the ore wagons, and the other half have been during the stage holdups. Mallory don't care. He's shot a driver, two guards, and four passengers."

"I imagine that hasn't been very good for the line's business," Longarm said dryly.

Willard nodded. "Folks are gettin' too spooked to ride the coaches unless they have to. And I can't say as I blame 'em, either."

"Well, I'll be riding the one tomorrow with that silver shipment." Longarm hefted the Winchester. "And if Ben Mallory comes calling, I'll do my best to give him one hell of a surprise."

Longarm ate supper with Willard at a hash house down the street, then the two of them came back to the station to wait for Angus Jenkins. Tonopah had quite a few saloons, and the sounds of music and laughter coming from them were a temptation, but Longarm didn't give in to it. Willard lit a fire in the stove to warm the place up, and the two of them sat and smoked and talked while night fell.

Jenkins showed up about an hour later. He was a rawboned Scotsman with a fiery red beard, a fierce countenance, and a burr so thick Longarm could only understand about half of what he was saying. He drove up to the back of the station in a wagon, and Willard blew out the lamp in the building when he and Longarm heard the squeak of the wheels. The office had a back door, and that was what the three men used as they each carried in a heavy carpetbag. Willard lit the lamp again.

The silver wasn't raw ore. It had been roughly refined and shaped into crude ingots. Longarm wasn't sure how much money this shipment represented; more than he made in several years' time, that was certain. Still, he didn't feel any particular temptation as he watched Willard and Jenkins pack the silver into the bottom of the mailbags that would be used the next day. He had long since learned that there were more important things in life than being rich.

"There's an extra cot in the tack room, Marshal," Willard said. "Why don't you stay here with me tonight so we can keep an eye on these bags?"

"That's just what I had in mind," agreed Longarm. "No point in worrying so much about tomorrow that we get careless tonight."

"Aye," rumbled Jenkins. He added something that was largely unintelligible, then laughed and slapped Longarm on the back. Longarm just grinned.

Longarm and Willard stayed up a while after Jenkins had left, then took turns standing guard over the silver all night. Willard stood the last watch so that Longarm could get some sleep before the coach bound for Carson City rolled in. When Longarm got up at dawn, he checked the mailbags to be sure that the silver hadn't been tampered with. Seeing Willard watching him, he said, "No offense, old son."

"Hell, none taken," the stationmaster replied. "If you'd had the last watch, I would've checked the bags myself. They say every man has his price."

"I reckon. I just hope nobody ever offers me mine, 'cause I'd hate to find out it was true."

The coach rolled into Tonopah a few minutes after seven. George was driving, and Pryor was riding shotgun again. They had spent the night in Goldfield, several miles south of Tonopah, and were now on the return trip to Carson City. Longarm drank some coffee brewed in a pot on Willard's stove, grabbed some biscuits from the hash house, and was ready to go when George picked up the reins and yelled at the team. This time, he was the only passenger.

The trip between Tonopah and Rawhide passed without any trouble. The stage stopped for lunch and a fresh team of horses at an isolated station northwest of Rawhide, then rolled on toward Carson City. With each mile that passed beneath the coach's wheels, Longarm grew more surprised that there had been no sign of trouble. From what Billy Vail had told him, nearly every stage that was carrying silver had been stopped during the past month. It was beginning to look as if this shipment was going to get through, though.

The stagecoach had barely rocked to a stop in front of the Carson City station when Longarm swung down through the door. Bat Thompson was waiting for him, and the stage-line owner didn't seem particularly surprised to see him. "Howdy," Thompson said. "Figured you'd make it all right."

"What do you mean?" asked Longarm. "I thought you were expecting trouble."

"That was before I heard about what happened up in Virginny City yesterday. Mallory was too busy shootin' up the place to even think about holdin' up this stage."

Longarm frowned. "Mallory attacked Virginia City?"

Thompson scratched at his beard and said, "I wouldn't call it an attack. What happened is, Mallory and some o' his

31

boys were in town, and a couple of vigilantes spotted 'em and tried to arrest 'em. Well, Mallory and his men shot those damn fools to doll rags, o' course, and took off into the mountains north of there with a posse after 'em. But Mallory gave those vigilantes the slip, slick as can be.'' The stage-line owner spat into the dust of the street and went on reluctantly. ''The worst thing about it is that somebody else got in the way of a bullet when all the shootin' started. She'd just got off the stage too when it happened.''

A wind colder than anything that blew over the Nevada wasteland seemed to freeze Longarm's blood in his veins. His jaw tightened. He stared at Thompson for a moment, then said, ''She?''

Thompson nodded. ''Yeah. She stopped by the office before she boarded the stage here and told me she was your friend. Miss Amelia Loftus, she said her name was.''

''And she was hit by a stray bullet?'' Longarm forced the words out. For some reason, he had to hear the truth spoken plain.

''I'm sorry, Marshal. I reckon she never knew what hit her.'' Thompson put a hand on Longarm's shoulder. ''She's dead.''

And it was Ben Mallory's fault, thought Longarm. Fate had twisted around on itself, and the very man Longarm had expected to see today over the sights of his rifle had instead been miles to the north, causing the death of a nice young woman who hadn't wanted anything except a little excitement in her life. Longarm's hands tightened on the rifle he was carrying. He had never met Ben Mallory, had never even seen the man.

But he would be mighty glad when the sorry son of a bitch was dead.

# Chapter 5

Virginia City was only about fifteen miles northeast of Carson City. Longarm got his saddle and warbag from the boot of the stagecoach and pitched the bag into Bat Thompson's office. "Keep an eye on that for me, will you?" he asked the stage-line owner.

Thompson nodded. "Sure. You headin' up to Virginny City?"

"That's the last place anybody saw Mallory, and everybody's convinced that he's the one behind the holdups. Seems like the best place to start." Longarm turned and headed down the street toward the nearest livery stable, carrying his saddle and rifle.

The sky had been clear earlier in the day, but now thick gray clouds were blowing in. That suited Longarm's mood just fine. He couldn't believe Amelia was dead. He had seen her only yesterday morning, he thought, had held her and kissed her and listened to her laugh.

And promised her that he would come see her in Virginia City.

The owner of the livery stable must have seen that Longarm was in no mood to haggle. He named a fair price for the rental of a horse, and Longarm picked out a rangy line-bred dun with a mean look in its eyes and a broad chest that

33

indicated it had plenty of stamina. He saddled the horse himself, ignoring the stablekeeper's offer of help, then led the dun back down the street to Bat Thompson's office.

Longarm used the tack room to change clothes, shedding the brown tweed suit in favor of denim pants, a work shirt, and a sheepskin jacket. If he was going to be riding, he wanted to be comfortable.

"Anything I can do to help, Marshal?" asked Thompson as Longarm prepared to mount.

Longarm swung up into the saddle and shook his head. "Chasing down owlhoots like Mallory is my job," he said.

"Well, good luck. I hope you catch the bastard."

So did Longarm. As he rode out of Carson City, he tried to tell himself that when he apprehended Ben Mallory, he would be professional about it. He was sworn to uphold the law, not to take it into his own hands. He couldn't just blow Mallory's head off in cold blood, no matter how much he wanted to every time he thought about what had happened to Amelia Loftus.

Of course, if Mallory resisted arrest, that was a whole 'nother matter . . .

Longarm grimaced and put that thought out of his head. First he had to get to Virginia City and hope that he could pick up the outlaw's trail.


Longarm had been to Virginia City before and recalled that the town was hard to see until a rider was almost on top of it. That hadn't changed. The settlement was surrounded by rocky hills dotted with scrubby pine trees. The hills gave way suddenly to a long, shallow valley where the predominant color was a sandy brown. That was due not only to the ground itself but to the thick layer of dust that lay over everything, deposited there by blasting from the mines. A few years earlier, during the so-called Big Bonanza, the ground had shaken almost constantly from the explosions. Now, the mines were not as active any longer, though many were still steady producers.

And Virginia City's main thoroughfare, C Street, was still busy night and day. At the moment, as night was falling, the street was clogged with wagons, pedestrians, and men on horseback, most of them bound for one of the many saloons that lined the avenue.

Longarm reined the dun to a stop in front of a small stone building with a sign out front that read City Marshal. He dismounted and tied the horse to the hitch rail along the boardwalk, then crossed to the door and opened it without knocking. A man stood near a potbellied stove in a corner of the room, extending his hands toward it to warm them. The man was somewhat potbellied, too, although his shoulders were thick with muscle, not fat. He had a mustache and dark brown hair that was shot through with gray, despite the fact that he was only thirty or so, Longarm estimated. A tin star was pinned to his leather vest.

The man gave Longarm a nod and said in a friendly voice, "Howdy. Something I can do for you?"

"You the city marshal, like it says outside?" Longarm knew his tone was a bit curt, but his mood hadn't improved any during the ride up here.

"That's right. Name's Everett Day."

"I'm a lawman, too. U.S. deputy marshal out of Denver." Longarm took out the folder containing his badge and bona fides and handed it to Day.

The town badge glanced at the identification papers and said, "Custis Long, eh? You'd be the one they call Longarm?"

"Some do," admitted Longarm. He was always a little surprised whenever he ran into someone who had heard of him. He didn't see any reason he should be famous, since he was just a fella doing what he'd signed on to do.

Day stuck out his hand and shook with Longarm. "Pleased to meet you. What can I do for you, Marshal?"

"I heard that Ben Mallory was here yesterday."

Day's beefy face lost its cheerful expression. "He sure as hell was. Killed two citizens and an unfortunate lady who had just arrived in town. Then he took off into the mountains. I gathered up some men and went after him but didn't have any luck," said Day with a rueful shake of his head. "Are you on that rascal's trail, too?"

"I'm told that he and his gang have been holding up stage-coaches in these parts." Longarm didn't know how much this local lawman might know about the silver shipments in the mailbags, so he kept that to himself. "I plan to stop him."

"Well, good luck to you, that's all I can say. Wish I could tell you where he's holed up. If I was you, I think I'd try Galena City first."

Longarm frowned. "Where's that? Don't reckon I've heard of it."

"It's a boomtown north of here about twenty miles. The place has gone boom and bust several times, in fact. Started out as a Mormon settlement called Hyrum, and after that some wag called it Doldrums. This latest silver boom gave it life again, and it was renamed Galena City. Galena's a mixture of silver and lead, you know, and I reckon that's a pretty apt description—silver from the mines and lead from all the bullets that go flyin' around. It's a wild place, from what I hear." Suddenly, Day lifted his hand and smacked himself lightly on the forehead with the base of his palm. "Hell, wouldn't you know it? I get to talking, and I forget all about my manners. You want some coffee, Longarm?"

The fella was talkative, all right, and so friendly that he didn't seem like he'd be much of a lawman. But that made him a good source of information, so Longarm said, "Sure. Coffee sounds good."

Day fetched cups for both of them and used a piece of leather to protect his hand as he picked up the pot that was simmering atop the stove. He poured Longarm's cup first and gestured for him to have a seat on the battered old sofa just inside the office door. Day took his cup behind the desk and sat down there in a simple ladderback chair.

Longarm sipped the coffee. It was bitter, but he had tasted

worse. "Hear you've got some vigilantes here helping you keep the peace," he commented.

Day grimaced. "I'd just as soon they'd keep their noses out of the law-and-order business," he said, "but what can you do when they're some of the most influential men in town? Still, if a couple of 'em hadn't decided to confront Ben Mallory themselves yesterday, instead of coming to tell me that he was in town, they'd still be alive now."

"And so would that woman," said Longarm.

Day nodded solemnly. "Yep, probably." Something about Longarm's voice must have alerted him to the fact that there was more to Longarm's words than a simple comment, because he leaned forward and added, "Did you have some connection with her, Marshal?"

"I knew her," Longarm said grimly. "I reckon you could say we were friends."

"Then I'm mighty sorry about what happened to the lady. We found a letter she'd written in her bag when it was unloaded from the stage. I take it she was Miss Amelia Loftus?"

Longarm nodded. "That's right. She was from Salt Lake City."

"Yes, sir, I know. The letter was to her folks there. I sent it on to them this morning, along with a note explaining what had happened. We, ah, had the funeral this morning, too."

Longarm's face was like granite as he nodded. "I'll be visiting your graveyard to pay my respects before I ride out in the morning."

"I'll take you out there myself."

"You say Mallory and his bunch headed for Galena City when they rode out of here?" Longarm forced his mind away from his memories of Amelia and back onto the job at hand.

"Well, they started in that general direction. That doesn't mean they went to Galena City."

"But that's where you'd start looking?"

Day hesitated, then gave a firm nod. "If I was you, Marshal, I sure would. Mallory's bunch has to be getting their

37

supplies from somewhere, and it's sure not here.''

Longarm drained the rest of the coffee from the cup and pushed himself to his feet. As he set the empty cup on the desk, he said, "Much obliged for the information."

"You're not pushing on to Galena City tonight, are you?"

"No, I reckon I'll get a hotel room—"

Before Longarm could finish his reply, the door of the office burst open and a man hurried in, his eyes wide with excitement. "There's trouble down at the Pioneer Saloon, Everett!" he exclaimed. "Looks like there's fixin' to be a brawl!"

Longarm glanced at the newcomer. He was a townie wearing a suit and a felt hat. A storekeeper, maybe, who had spotted the trouble he was reporting while he was on his way home to his family.

"A brawl, huh?" repeated Day. He didn't sound particularly alarmed, nor did he seem to be in any hurry as he put his palms on the desk and pushed himself to his feet. "Well, we can't have that, Johnny, so thanks for letting me know about it. I'll go down there and see if I can sort out the trouble." He smiled at Longarm as he reached for his hat. "Be glad to point out a good hotel to you if you want to walk part of the way with me."

Day was liable to be walking into more trouble than he expected, thought Longarm. "I'll go with you," he said. "Could be you might need a hand."

"Well, I sure appreciate that." Day settled his hat on his head and walked toward the door. "I'll be glad for the company."

Longarm left the dun tied up at the rail and walked alongside Day down C Street. Day pointed out the International Hotel, a five-story structure of brick and stone that was probably the biggest building in Virginia City. "Best place in town to hang your hat while you're here," said Day.

The townie who had burst into the marshal's office trailed along behind Longarm and Day, obviously eager to see what was going to happen. Day headed for the Pioneer, a good-sized saloon whose front took up half a block. The doors were closed against the chilly night air.

Longarm and Day were still several yards from the entrance when a man came sailing through the big front window, shattering the plate glass into a million pieces.

Day stopped short and said, "Good Lord. Johnny was right. There *is* trouble here."

That seemed pretty damned obvious to Longarm. His instincts told him to get in there before somebody else got thrown through the window. But this was Day's town, so he reined in the impulse and told himself to follow the local lawman's lead.

Day went to the man who was lying half on the low boardwalk and half in the street. He bent over him and asked, "That you, Phil? Are you all right?"

The man mumbled something. Longarm caught a name—Garvin.

Day helped the man called Phil to his feet and gave him a gentle push toward the townie who had reported the fight. "Johnny, see that Phil gets home all right, would you?"

"But Everett," protested the townie, "I was hoping—"

"Now, just go along like I asked you," Day said mildly. "I'd take it as a personal favor."

"All right, all right." Johnny grasped Phil's arm. "Come on, Phil. Let's go."

Day turned toward the saloon's front door and said to Longarm, "Jake Garvin is the bouncer in here. He fancies himself a tough man, and he likes to prove it. Sometimes he provokes trouble just so he can toss somebody through that window." Day sighed. "If I was LeClerc, the fella who owns this place, I'd take the cost of replacing that glass out of Jake's wages about half the time. But I reckon LeClerc's scared of Jake, too. I should have put a stop to this a long time ago."

"I'll back your play, Marshal, whatever you want to do," Longarm told him.

39

"Thanks." Day grinned. "I'll holler if I need a hand, so you be ready, Longarm."

If it had been him, thought Longarm, he would have gone into the place with a gun already in his hand. But Day just opened the door and strolled in. Raucous laughter filled the air, along with tobacco smoke and the smells of stale beer and unwashed human flesh. In short, it smelled like every other saloon Longarm had ever been in.

The laughter came from the bar, where a tall, burly man with a bald, bullet-shaped head was holding court. That would be Jake Garvin, Longarm speculated, and the guess was confirmed as Garvin began to explain how he had grabbed hold of Phil and thrown him through the window. That brought more howls of laughter from the sycophants around him. A few feet away along the bar, a small, dapper man stood with a worried look on his face. Longarm pegged him as LeClerc, the owner of the saloon, who right about now was undoubtedly regretting the fact that he had ever hired Garvin.

The other folks in the saloon were quiet for the most part, so the silence was thick when Garvin and his cronies saw Day striding toward them and stopped laughing. Garvin glowered at the local lawman and said, "What do *you* want, Day?"

"That's Marshal Day, Jake, and you know what I want. I've spoken to you before about causing trouble—"

"I didn't cause nothin'!" Garvin broke in heatedly. "That bastard started the whole thing!" A chorus of agreement came from the men around Garvin.

"He did?" said Day. "That's odd. Phil's usually a pretty peaceable sort. What did he do, Jake?"

"Why, he . . . he sat in my chair, that's what he did!"

Day nodded. "I see. So, naturally, you had to pitch him out of the window for doing that."

"Damn right! He got what he deserved, didn't he, boys?"

"I'm afraid that doesn't sound justified to me, Jake," Day said with a shake of his head. He stepped forward and reached out with his left hand to grasp Garvin's right arm. "You'll have to come with me and explain things to the judge in the morning. I'm locking you up."

Longarm had tensed as Day approached Garvin. The big man looked just as astounded by Day's audacity as Longarm was. But the surprise faded quickly from Garvin's face, to be replaced by a twisted expression of rage.

"You crazy son of a bitch!" he bellowed at Day. "Don't you know who I am?"

"You're a man who's going to jail," replied Day. "Come along now."

Longarm saw Garvin's shoulders twitch and knew the man was about to throw a punch. Garvin moved fast for such a big man. His left fist whipped up and around in a crushing blow.

Unfortunately for Garvin, the punch never landed. Day leaned back just far enough for Garvin's fist to pass harmlessly in front of his face. Then Day stepped in even closer and hooked a punch of his own into Garvin's midsection. Day's right fist didn't move much more than a foot, but the blow packed enough power to make Garvin gasp and start to double over. He couldn't bend, though, because Day's left hand was still holding him up. Day chopped another right into Garvin's face, striking so fast that it was difficult to follow his movements.

Longarm started to grin as Garvin's body sagged in Day's grip. Appearances could sometimes be mighty damned deceiving.

Then Longarm's right hand flashed across his body and palmed out the Colt from his cross-draw rig. He had the revolver leveled and cocked in less than the blink of an eye. The barrel of the gun was pointed at one of Garvin's cronies, who had started to draw his pistol behind Day's back.

"I wouldn't do that, old son," said Longarm quietly.

Day glanced over his shoulder. Garvin was no longer a threat, being half-senseless from the clubbing blows he had received. Day smiled at Longarm and said, "Thanks. I was

41

about to turn around, but you've saved me the trouble.'' He started toward the front door of the saloon, hauling Garvin along with him. Garvin stumbled, but Day held him up with seeming effortlessness. He shoved Garvin out the door.

The man who had been about to draw his gun stared at Longarm. He was pale, and he licked his lips nervously. He let go of the gun and allowed it to slide back into its holster.

''That's better,'' said Longarm. ''Now leave it there.''

One of the would-be gunman's companions punched him on the arm and said, ''You damned idiot! You're lucky that stranger took a hand. If he hadn't, Day probably would've killed you!''

''Yeah.'' The man took a deep breath. He was positively ashen now as he thought about his close call. He looked at Longarm and added, ''Sorry, mister.''

Longarm let down the hammer of his Colt and holstered it. He had misjudged Everett Day, all right.

''I don't take kindly to backshooters,'' he warned the men at the bar.

''You don't have to worry about us, mister,'' one of them said. ''We don't want any trouble with the marshal.''

Clearly, Day had a better grip on this town than Longarm had thought. He went to the door and stepped out into the frigid night. What Day had said earlier haunted him. If the men who had spotted Mallory had gone to the marshal instead of trying to confront the outlaws themselves, Longarm's job might be over now. Mallory might be either dead or behind bars.

And Amelia might still be alive.

Longarm squared his shoulders and headed back down the street. The sound of hammering followed him. Somebody was already nailing boards over the broken window in the saloon.

42

# Chapter 6

A cold wind plucked at Longarm's hat and coat the next morning as he stood on the small hill where Virginia City's graveyard was located. The winds in these parts were called Washoe Zephyrs, he remembered, a term that was both a tribute to the Washoe Valley and an ironic comment on the strength of the winds. Despite the chill in the air, he reached up and plucked his hat off in a gesture of respect as he looked at the new grave marker and the mound of freshly turned earth.

Amelia's name was burned into the wood of the marker, along with the date of her death. That was all the undertaker had known about her. He hadn't known anything about her dissatisfaction with the life for which she seemed to be destined, or her thirst for adventure, or the way she laughed, or how sweet her mouth had tasted . . .

"I'm sorry, Amelia," Longarm said aloud. "I wish I'd been able to keep my promise to come see you earlier. But I'm here now, and I'm making you another promise. I'll track down the skunks who did this, and I'll see to it that they pay."

"Amen," said Everett Day. The Virginia City marshal had brought Longarm up here and showed him the grave, and

43

now he stood a few feet behind Longarm, also holding his hat in his hand respectfully.

"I'd like to get that marker replaced with a permanent headstone," said Longarm as he turned away from the grave. "Better wait until you hear from her folks, though. They can tell you what ought to be on there."

"They may want to pay for it," Day pointed out.

Longarm shook his head. "Tell the undertaker to send the bill to me at the chief marshal's office in Denver. I'll take care of it."

Day fell in step beside Longarm as the tall lawman started down the hill toward C Street. "I'll tell him," Day said. Both men put their hats on.

"Is there a road from here to Galena City?"

"Sure. It goes from here to Galena City and then on up to Reno. You can take it, or you can circle around to the east and hit the old trail the Mormons, who settled the place, used, and come in that way."

"I want to get there as soon as possible," said Longarm.

Day nodded. "Then you want the new road. Go on over to A Street and follow it out of town. When you get to the end of it, keep going."

"Much obliged."

"You got plenty of supplies? If not, there are several stores here where you can stock up."

"I reckon I can make it all right," said Longarm. He got the impression that Marshal Day didn't much want him to leave town. Maybe Day was a little worried about what might happen when he let Jake Garvin out of jail and wanted Longarm around to lend him a hand. But having seen the way Day could take care of himself the night before, Longarm didn't really think that was the answer.

Still, he asked idly, "What's going to happen with Garvin?"

Day shrugged his thick shoulders. "Judge'll fine him and turn him loose."

44

"Is he liable to try to even the score with you for throwing him in jail?"

"I doubt it," Day said with a short laugh. "Jake and I have had our share of run-ins before. He always forgets from one time to the next that he usually winds up with the short end of the stick. Don't worry about Jake, Longarm. He'll be peaceable for a while now, until he gets it in his head again that he's the cock of the roost around here."

"And when he does, you'll point out to him that he's wrong," said Longarm.

"That's my job."

They had reached the livery stable where Longarm had left the dun the night before. He stopped and turned to Day, extending his hand. "I've enjoyed meeting you, Marshal," he said, "and I'm much obliged for all your help."

Day shook hands with Longarm and sighed. "I got to admit, there's a big part of me wishing I could go along with you, Longarm. I'd like to see Ben Mallory and his boys get what's coming to them."

So that was it. Day didn't particularly want Longarm to stay in Virginia City; he just wished he could go along with the federal man. Longarm nodded and said, "Mallory and his gang will get what's coming to them, all right. You can count on that."

"You know," said Day, "I believe I can."

The trail from Virginia City to Galena City was narrow but not too small to accommodate stagecoaches, so anyone who wanted to ship silver from Galena City could send it to Virginia City on one of Bat Thompson's coaches and then on to Carson City. From there, the railroad linked Carson City to the rest of the country.

Longarm wondered if Mallory's gang had carried out any robberies in these parts. The gang had hit the stages traveling between Virginia City and Carson City several times, according to Everett Day, but the local lawman hadn't said anything about trouble in this direction, other than the fact

45

that Galena City was supposed to be a pretty wild place.

Which meant it might make a good headquarters for a bunch like Mallory's, reflected Longarm. Some of these boomtowns came and went so fast that no real law ever had a chance to be established. There might not be any badge-toters in Galena City to represent a threat to Mallory, not even a vigilante group.

But he was getting ahead of himself, he supposed. Since it was impossible to eat an apple more than one bite at a time, he'd just have to wait until he reached Galena City to find out what the situation was there.

Thick gray clouds scudded through the sky above Long-arm, and sometimes he had trouble determining where the clouds began and the craggy mountain peaks ended. The ride took several hours, and it was well past noon by the time he came in sight of Galena City. His stomach was rumbling from hunger, but he decided it would be better to wait and get something to eat in the settlement. Ironically, considering what he had been told about the place, the first thing he saw was the spire of a church steeple. So there was a little bit of heaven to be found here, to go along with all the hell.

The town was built at the end of a valley that opened up to east and west at its northern tip, so it was laid out in the shape of a large T. The road Longarm was on turned into the main north-south street, which he saw from a sign tacked onto a post as he was entering the settlement was called Greenwood Avenue. The church was at the southern end of this street, on the right, and as Longarm rode past, he saw that the building was rather dilapidated. It might still be in use, or it might be just a vestige of the town's Mormon origins. Longarm couldn't tell.

The rest of Galena City was bustling, though. Many of the buildings were new, and even the older ones had fresh coats of paint. New boards had replaced older, rotted ones in the sidewalks in front of the buildings. Several wagons were parked along both sides of the street, and horses were tied up at most of the hitch racks. People hurried along the boardwalks and went in and out of stores, and none of them paid much attention at all to the tall stranger riding down Greenwood Avenue. Longarm figured that the sight of a newcomer was nothing unusual to them. Folks came and went all the time in a boomtown.

He saw several general mercantiles, a hardware store, the stagecoach station, a saddle shop, a gunsmith and a blacksmith, an apothecary, even a newspaper office where the Galena City *Bugle* was published. But he didn't see a marshal's office or a jail, which confirmed his guess that this incarnation of Galena City was too new to have any real law and order. The citizens here would have to solve their own problems as they arose.

Though most of the people he saw were roughly dressed men, there were a few females on the boardwalks, too, and he could tell from their dark, sober dresses and coats and bonnets that they were respectable women, probably the wives and daughters of mine superintendents or owners. If he had been married, thought Longarm, he wouldn't have brought his wife to a place like this. But since it was pretty damned unlikely he would ever settle down and get hitched, he supposed he didn't have any right to make a judgment like that. He'd had enough experience with women to know that it was pretty near impossible to say no to them once they had their mind made up.

Amelia Loftus, for example.

Longarm's mouth tightened at that thought. He looked more closely at the men he was passing on the street. He had only a rough description of Ben Mallory, and almost any of the men he saw in Galena City could have been the outlaw leader.

When he drew even with the newspaper office, Longarm veered his horse to the side of the street and reined to a stop. He swung down and looped the reins over the hitch rack. If the editor was in the office, that ink-stained wretch would be as good a place as any to start.

"Afternoon," Longarm said as he stepped into the newspaper office and shut the door behind him. A short wooden fence with a gate in it divided the single large room. A man stood on the other side of the fence next to a printing press. Judging from the angry expression on his face and the hammer he clutched tightly in his hand, he was having trouble with the press.

The man confirmed that by striking the machine a ringing blow with the hammer. "Damned thing!" he said. "I ought to load you in a wagon and tumble you off into a ravine somewhere!" He glanced at Longarm. "What do you want?"

Well, that wasn't the friendliest greeting he'd ever gotten, Longarm thought. He said, "I reckon you're the editor here?"

"Publisher, editor, salesman, and I sweep out the place and empty the slops jar." The man hit the press again with the hammer. "And wrestle weekly with this ungodly piece of the Devil's machinery." He threw the hammer aside in disgust and turned to face Longarm. "J. Emerson Dupree at your service, sir."

"Name's Custis," said Longarm, leaving off the second half of his handle just in case this fella Dupree was another one who had heard of him. "I need a little information, I reckon."

"Then why in the name of all that's holy would you come to a newspaper? You'd be better off inquiring of the lowest drunk writhing in the gutter."

Longarm couldn't help but chuckle. Some folks were so bitter and cynical that he couldn't quite take them seriously. J. Emerson Dupree appeared to fall into that category.

The newspaperman was short and stocky, with gray hair and a neatly pointed beard. He wore black trousers and a black vest over a white shirt, and the clothes were protected by a long, ink-stained canvas apron. The sleeves of his shirt were rolled up over muscular forearms. His hands had splotches of ink on them, too. His bushy eyebrows were drawn down in a frown as he glowered at Longarm and demanded, "Do you find me amusing, sir?"

"Nope," Longarm lied, "it's just that I've had to handle mules that were just as balky as that printing press of yours, Mr. Dupree. I reckon I know how you must feel right about now. You want the loan of my Colt so's you can shoot that infernal machine a time or two?"

Dupree sighed. "No, I suppose that wouldn't do any good. I can get the damned contraption working again with a little time and patience—two items of which I'm in short supply. So whatever you want, spit it out, man."

"I'm told there's silver in these parts," said Longarm. "Is that true?"

Dupree rolled his eyes. "Didn't you see the headframes of the mines on the slopes above the settlement as you rode in? I wouldn't go so far as to say this field will be another Comstock Lode, but yes, there is silver to be had in this area."

"Good. I thought I might try my hand at mining." Longarm put a worried frown on his face. "But I've heard tell that some gang of robbers has been stealing a lot of the silver shipments. What about that? Any truth to the rumor?"

Instantly, Dupree's expression changed. Longarm saw the nervousness come into the man's eyes. "I don't know what you're talking about," he said gruffly.

"You being a newspaperman, I figured you'd have heard the stories—"

"Well, I haven't," Dupree cut in. He flapped his ink-stained hands. "Nothing to it, as far as I know. Now, if that's all . . ." He turned back toward the press, clearly dismissing Longarm from his thoughts.

Longarm wasn't going to give up that easily. He said, "What about the law? Is there a marshal or sheriff around here?"

Without looking around, Dupree snorted in contempt. "This was a ghost town until six months ago, mister. The

49

nearest law is in either Virginia City or Reno, depending on which direction you want to go.''

''You mean there's not even a vigilance committee?''

''People are too busy to worry themselves with such nonsense.''

''Well,'' said Longarm, ''I don't know if I want to settle here or not. I'm the mild-mannered sort, you know. Don't care for trouble.''

''Then you're in the wrong damned place, all right,'' snapped Dupree. He bent over and picked up his hammer, then glanced over his shoulder in annoyance. ''Look, I'm busy. Is there anything else?''

The rumble of Longarm's stomach reminded him that he still hadn't eaten. He asked, ''Where can a fella get a good surrounding of chuck?''

Dupree gestured with the hammer. ''Four doors down on the left. The Chinaman's place.'' The newspaperman's surly attitude eased a little as he went on. ''It's simple fare, fried steaks and potatoes for the most part, but you won't find much better around here.''

Longarm tugged on the brim of his hat. ''Much obliged. I reckon I'll see you around, Mr. Dupree . . . if I decide to stay in Galena City.''

''Doesn't matter to me one way or the other.'' Dupree's next words were punctuated with grunts and the sound of the hammer striking the printing press. ''Never—uh!—should've listened—uh!—to that damned Greeley!''

# Chapter 7

J. Emerson Dupree had been right about one thing, Longarm reflected a little later: the food in the Chinaman's place wasn't bad. The steak that the pigtailed gent set down on the counter in front of Longarm was fried up nice and tender, and the potatoes weren't swimming in grease.

But Dupree had been lying about something else, and Longarm knew it. The newspaperman was well aware of the ore-wagon robberies and stagecoach holdups that had taken place in the area. Longarm had seen that knowledge in his eyes, along with the nervousness.

What was Dupree scared of? Why hadn't he wanted to admit that he had heard about Mallory's gang?

Longarm looked up and nodded to the Chinaman. "This is good," he said with a smile.

The place was little more than a narrow hole-in-the-wall with a counter, a couple of tables, and a kitchen in the back where a woman and several youngsters, no doubt the Chinaman's wife and kids, scurried about. The Chinaman himself delivered the platters of food to the customers. Even though it was past lunchtime, the room was full, and Longarm had been lucky to get a seat at the counter. Having sampled the fare, Longarm wasn't surprised at the popularity of the establishment.

At the moment, the Chinaman was standing behind the counter with his arms crossed, and he accepted Longarm's compliment with a curt nod. He didn't return the lawman's smile.

"Looks like you're doing a booming business," Longarm went on. He wasn't going to give up just yet. "The whole town's pretty busy, from what I've seen of it."

"You want more food?" asked the Chinaman.

Longarm hadn't eaten more than half of what was on his plate. "Maybe in a few minutes," he said. "I guess that's why they call it a boomtown, ain't it, because business is booming."

The Chinaman looked off to one side, deliberately ignoring him.

"Having a gang of bandits in the area doesn't seem to have hurt the town," Longarm said.

He was rewarded with a flick of the Chinaman's eyes and a look of alarm that passed across the man's face so quickly that Longarm might have imagined it. He hadn't, though. For a second there, the Chinaman had looked scared, just like J. Emerson Dupree in the newspaper office down the street.

The man sitting next to Longarm wasn't as self-controlled as the Celestial behind the counter. He grunted, looked over at Longarm, and asked, "What did you say, mister?"

Longarm turned to him with a guileless smile. "I said that having a bunch of outlaws in these parts doesn't seem to have hurt Galena City any."

"Outlaws, you say?"

Longarm nodded and said, "If you're from around here, you must have heard the stories about a fella called Mallory, or something like that."

From the corner of his eye, Longarm saw the Chinaman react to Mallory's name. Although he quickly banished the expression again, for a second the Chinaman looked positively queasy. He didn't like all this talk about outlaws in his place. He especially didn't like the fact that Longarm had mentioned Ben Mallory.

52

The man sitting next to Longarm said harshly, "I've heard a lot of things I don't go around yappin' about."

Longarm acted surprised. "I didn't mean no offense, mister. I'm just new to these parts, and I'm trying to figure out if it'd be safe to maybe settle here."

"Keep your mouth shut and your nose out of other people's business and you'll be safe enough." The man drained the last of the coffee from his cup, tossed a coin on the counter to pay for his meal, and started to stand up.

Longarm swiveled on the rough wooden stool where he was sitting. He reached out and put a hand on the man's arm. "I said I was sorry, old son. I didn't know you were friends with this fella Mallory—"

The man shook off Longarm's hand. "My friends are my business," he growled. "And I never said Mallory was one of 'em. It's just that *I've* got some sense."

Longarm stood up too and faced the man. "You've got no call to insult me," he said. He wasn't really that offended, but now that he had finally gotten a rise out of somebody by mentioning Mallory's name, he didn't want to let go of a possible lead.

"Please, no trouble in here," the Chinaman said quickly. He came out from behind the counter and tried to get between Longarm and the other man. "You want argue, go outside, please."

The other man was almost as tall as Longarm and was broader through the body and shoulders than the lawman. He took hold of the Chinaman and easily moved him aside. "If you don't like what I've got to say," he snapped at Longarm, "you can do something about it, mister."

Longarm prodded back verbally, saying, "Why don't you just go tell your pard Mallory—"

That was as far as he got. The other man said loudly, "Mallory's not my pard! I hate the son of a bitch!"

Then he swung his big right fist straight at Longarm's head.

Longarm saw the punch coming and ducked to let it go

over him. Thrown off balance by the missed blow, the man stumbled forward a step. That brought him close enough for Longarm to put a fist into his belly. The man grunted but was rocked only slightly by the punch. He roared and threw his arms around Longarm, catching the lawman in a bear hug.

With both of his arms trapped, Longarm had no choice but to bring his knee up into his opponent's groin. That brought a howl of pain from the man, and his grip loosened. Longarm tore free, threw a left and a right that landed on the man's jaw, jerking his head back and forth. The man staggered back and fell as the other patrons of the Chinaman's place scrambled to get out of his way. One of the tables went over with a crash, and the Chinaman let out an outraged screech. Longarm glanced around to make sure the Celestial wasn't coming after him with a cleaver. He had faced hatchet men before and had no desire to do so again.

The Chinaman was just jumping up and down and yelling, though, so Longarm didn't figure he was much of a threat. Longarm bent over, grabbed the coat of the man he had knocked down, and hauled him to his feet.

"Sorry that had to happen, friend," Longarm said to the man, who was shaking his head groggily. "I didn't want any trouble."

The man pulled away from Longarm. With a snarl, he reached down and picked up his hat, which had come off when he fell. "You're liable to get more than you can handle, you keep runnin' your mouth off like that," he said. He clapped the hat on his head and said to the Chinaman, "You can take up the matter of damages with this fella here, Ling." He pointed at Longarm, then turned on his heel and stalked out of the little restaurant.

Ling was still furious, though he was clearly glad that the fight was over. He pointed at the overturned table and said to Longarm, "You break table, spill food! Must pay!" He held up his hand with the fingers spread. "Five dolla'."

Longarm figured that no more than a dollar's worth of

food had wound up on the floor, and as for the table, it would be just fine as soon as somebody set it upright again. But he didn't feel like arguing, so he dug in the pocket of his jeans and pulled out a five-dollar gold piece. He flipped it to Ling, who plucked it deftly from the air and bit into it, then nodded in satisfaction.

"Sorry," Longarm said. He looked around at the other customers in the narrow room. "Sorry, folks. I didn't know I was touching a sore spot when I brought up that outlaw Mallory."

Several of the men in the room looked down at the floor. Others shifted their feet. One man cleared his throat. "We don't know who you're talkin' about, mister," he said. "There's nobody by that name around here."

The hell there wasn't, thought Longarm. He was beginning to understand now. His guess about Galena City being without a lawman had proven to be correct, and that led to his next theory.

Ben Mallory had this town treed.

Longarm had seen situations like this before. A group of badmen moved in on a settlement, usually somewhat isolated and without anybody to keep the peace, and took over. In return for a safe haven where they could replenish their supplies and indulge their appetites for liquor and women of easy virtue, they left everybody in the town alone, at least for the most part. As long as they weren't crossed, that is. If somebody got brave enough to stand up to them, the owlhoots would slap him down ruthlessly, sometimes even killing him as a lesson to everybody else. So, for their own good, the townspeople went along with whatever the outlaws wanted.

That was Galena City.

So if he waited, thought Longarm, sooner or later Ben Mallory would come to him, especially if Longarm kept stirring up the townsfolk with his comments. Mallory was bound to hear about that. There was only one problem with that plan.

Longarm didn't feel like waiting. He wanted Mallory—
*now*.

He nodded to the customers in the Chinaman's place, who
pointedly ignored him as he walked out. With his belly full,
Longarm felt pretty good. He paused on the boardwalk to
light a cheroot, then strolled along Greenwood Avenue toward the intersection where it hit the other main street.

He had only gone a block and was passing the mouth of
an alley when he heard someone go, "Sssttt!"

Longarm frowned and glanced over at the alley. J. Emerson Dupree stood there motioning to him. The newspaper
publisher had taken off his ink-stained apron and put on a
dusty black coat and derby hat. He glanced around furtively
as he called Longarm over to him, as if he was afraid that
someone would see him.

The overcast sky was still thick with clouds, which meant
the alley was shadowy, but Longarm could see well enough
to be sure that no one was in there except Dupree. This
certainly didn't look like an ambush, he told himself. He
decided to see what the newspaperman wanted.

Longarm stepped into the alley and nodded to Dupree.
"Howdy," he said around the cheroot clenched between his
teeth. "You were right about the Chinaman's place. The food
was good."

"Why didn't you just eat it and keep your mouth shut,
then?" asked Dupree. Before Longarm could answer, the
newspaperman went on. "I heard about what you just did in
there. That's why I scrambled around here to talk to you.
What are you trying to do, mister, get this town burned down
around us?"

"Mallory's got you that scared, huh?" Longarm asked
bluntly.

Dupree swallowed hard. "Who are you? Some kind of
bounty hunter, maybe?"

Longarm glanced around. There were no windows nearby
in the buildings, and even if there had been, they would have
been closed to keep the chill out. He decided to take a chance

56

and reveal who he really was to Dupree. He reached up, took the cheroot out of his mouth.

At the far end of the alley, a gun blasted. Something whined past Longarm's ear with a sound like an angry bee.

A .44-caliber bee, more than likely.

Longarm reacted instinctively. He dropped the cheroot and twisted around in the direction the shot had come from, and his hand flashed to the Colt in the cross-draw rig on his left hip. As the gun slid smoothly from its holster, another shot rang out. Longarm heard that whining sound again, followed by an ugly thud and a grunt of pain. He threw himself to the side, sprawling out flat on the ground next to one of the buildings, as he brought up the Colt and started triggering.

Three shots thundered out of the revolver, deafening in the close confines. The shadowy figure Longarm had spotted at the far end of the alley jerked back. As the echoes of Longarm's shots died away, he heard the sound of rapid footsteps on hard-packed dirt. The bushwhacker was getting away. Longarm thought he might have wounded the man—or maybe the ambusher had jerked because he was just getting out of the way of the lawman's bullets as fast as he could.

Someone moaned, and Longarm looked back over his shoulder to see J. Emerson Dupree lying in the alley. The newspaperman was on his back, and there was a large stain on his shirt that wasn't ink this time.

Longarm scrambled to his feet and then knelt beside Dupree. He pulled the man's coat and shirt back and saw the ugly, red-rimmed hole just below Dupree's left shoulder. There was probably a matching hole in Dupree's back, Longarm knew, where the bullet had come out. The wound was messy, but with any luck, it might not be fatal. From the looks of it, the slug had missed anything vital.

That knowledge didn't make Longarm feel any better. He knew the bullet had been meant for him. Dupree had been hit by accident. And Longarm was fairly confident that the ambush wouldn't have taken place if he hadn't ridden into town and started asking questions about Ben Mallory.

That was one more mark against the outlaw leader, Longarm told himself.

"Hang on, Dupree," Longarm told the newspaperman. He looked up at the sound of more running footsteps. "Folks are on their way to see what happened. Somebody will be here in a minute to help you."

Dupree couldn't hear him. He was only half-conscious, muttering and groaning in pain. Longarm glanced toward the far end of the alley where the bushwhacker had disappeared. The gunman didn't have a big lead on him, and if the man really was injured, that would slow him down even more. Besides, Longarm didn't much want to hang around here and have to answer questions about what had happened. He probably would have, if Galena City had had a real lawman, but under the circumstances, it might be better for him to get out of this alley while he had the chance.

He patted Dupree on the uninjured shoulder, muttered, "Sorry, old son," and stood up. His long legs carried him quickly to the far end of the alley. The Colt was still in his hand, ready for instant use.

Nobody was lurking at the end of the alley, though. Longarm stepped out into a lane that ran behind the buildings along Greenwood Avenue. He looked to his left, and a couple of blocks away saw a man hurriedly climbing onto a horse that was tied behind a building. Longarm started in that direction at a run, yelling, "Hey! Hold it right there!"

The man thumped down awkwardly in the saddle and twisted toward Longarm. Longarm saw the rifle in the man's hands, saw the barrel swinging up to point toward him. He dove to the side, landing behind a rain barrel. The rifle cracked and a slug punched through the barrel. Water spurted out on both sides. Longarm felt the stream splashing on the back of his coat.

He poked the Colt around the barrel and fired twice. That emptied the cylinder, and he had to pull back behind the barrel to reload. There was a handful of fresh cartridges in his coat pocket. He pulled them out, dumped the empties from the cylinder, and thumbed the new bullets in. By that time, hoofbeats filled the cold air, coming closer with each passing second.

The bushwhacker was charging him on horseback. The man's rifle barked again, and the bullet smacked into the rain barrel. Longarm forced himself to wait—not an easy thing to do when some son of a bitch was trying to kill him. Then, when he judged the time was right, he rose up and put his left shoulder against the barrel, pushing hard as he surged to his feet. The barrel tipped over, the lid coming off as it fell so that the water inside splashed out into the lane. The sudden flood was enough by itself to spook the ambusher's mount, but when the now-empty barrel rolled into its path, the horse shied violently, rearing up on its hind legs. The bushwhacker yelled in alarm and grabbed for the saddle horn.

Longarm drew a bead and shot the man in the right shoulder.

At least, that was where he was aiming. The horse danced to the side at the same instant Longarm pressed the trigger, and the lawman's bullet tore into the bushwhacker's chest instead and threw him out of the saddle. He landed hard, limbs sprawling limply. The frightened horse bolted down the lane, forcing Longarm to spring aside to avoid being trampled.

He hurried to the side of the fallen gunman. The man's breathing was harsh and labored. Blood trickled from the corner of his mouth. Longarm went to one knee beside him and said urgently, "You're hit bad, mister. Why don't you tell me why you were trying to kill me while you still can?"

The man looked up at Longarm with unfocused eyes. "B-bastard," he gasped. "You . . . you killed me!"

"Just returning the favor in advance," said Longarm grimly. "Who are you? Why'd you try to ambush me?"

The dying man grated out another curse, then in a voice that was rapidly weakening said, "Mallory would've . . . let me ride with him . . . if I'd ki—"

Blood gushed from the man's mouth, choking off whatever else he had meant to say. His eyes went glassy in death, and his head dropped to the side.

He had said enough before he died, though. Judging by his clothes, he was a miner or some sort of laborer, but he had clearly aspired to be more. He had wanted to be an outlaw, a member of Ben Mallory's gang, and he had thought that killing a suspicious stranger would be his ticket into Mallory's bunch. Longarm grimaced. He had expected his blunt questions to make him a target, but he had hoped the attempt would come from Mallory himself, not some would-be desperado eager to make a mark.

Longarm stood and holstered his Colt. He heard shouting nearby and knew that some of the townspeople would arrive in a matter of seconds. It was time for him to fade out of this picture, at least for the time being. He stepped into another alley, walked swiftly along it, and emerged on Greenwood Avenue once more. He found himself on the boardwalk in front of a hardware store, so he stepped inside.

The proprietor was the only one in the store, standing behind a counter in the rear. He looked nervous—like just nearly everyone else in Galena City—as he called to Longarm, "You know what's goin' on out there, mister? I heard shots and all sorts of runnin' around."

Longarm shook his head. "Afraid I wouldn't know, friend," he said. "You see, I'm the peaceable sort, and I stay as far away from trouble as I can."

# Chapter 8

Longarm stayed in the hardware store for a while, poking around at the items on the shelves. He didn't want to buy a pickax or a shovel or an auger, though, and when the store-keeper began to get really anxious, Longarm just said, "Much obliged," and stepped back out onto the boardwalk. He saw several groups of men standing around on both sides of the street, talking animatedly, but that was the only sign that anything had happened recently. The creaking of wheels drew Longarm's attention, and he looked over to see a wagon moving slowly along Greenwood Avenue. A man in a black suit and a tall hat was handling the reins, and a blanket-draped shape was in the back of the wagon. The local undertaker was already hauling off the man Longarm had killed.

He wondered about J. Emerson Dupree, wondered as well if there was a doctor here in Galena City. He waited until a woman was passing him on the boardwalk, then reached up and tugged on the brim of his hat as he said, "Pardon me, ma'am. Could you tell me if there's a sawbones in this town?"

She was a middle-aged woman with graying dark hair under her bonnet. Her gaze played over Longarm, and she said, "You look healthy enough, sir." He thought he saw just a hint of flirtatiousness in her eyes, so he grinned at her.

"I hope I am, ma'am," he said, "but you never can tell what's going to happen in the future."

"That's true enough," said the woman. "Unfortunately, there's no doctor here, just an old granny who serves as midwife and patches up bullet wounds."

"How is she at that?"

"Which one, midwifery or bullet wounds?"

Longarm chuckled. "I ain't likely to need a midwife any time soon, ma'am."

"In that case, I'm told she's quite efficient at cleaning and bandaging bullet holes."

Longarm tipped his hat again and said, "I'll keep that in mind. I'm obliged for the information, ma'am."

So there was at least a chance Dupree was in good hands, thought Longarm as he moved on down the street. He hated to think that the newspaperman might die simply because he had been in the wrong place at the wrong time, talking to Longarm.

But then, folks hardly ever died from being in the right place at the right time, he mused.

His horse was still tied in front of the newspaper office. He got the dun and led it down to the livery stable, where an old hostler took Longarm's money and put the horse in a stall. "We'll take good care of him," he promised.

Longarm nodded and asked, "Where's the nearest hotel?"

The hostler pointed out the open double doors of the barn. "Right across the street. Place is called Kingman's."

"Much obliged." Longarm had taken his Winchester from the saddle boot on the dun. He carried the rifle and his war-bag with him as he crossed the street toward the hotel, a two-story frame building made of thick, whitewashed planks.

Kingman's Hotel wasn't nearly as fancy inside as the International in Virginia City, but it would do for his needs, Longarm decided as he crossed the lobby. The floor at least had a rug on it, and several padded armchairs that weren't too broken-down were scattered around the room. A clerk with hair that was slicked down with pomade and parted in the middle stood behind the registration desk. He gave Longarm a professional smile and said, "Howdy-do. You want a room?"

"That's the idea," said Longarm with a nod. "Something quiet."

"That's a mite hard to come by in a place like Galena City," the clerk told him. "But I can put you on the second floor, rear. That'll get you as far away from the street as possible. Room'll run you two dollars a night."

Longarm frowned. "Pretty steep, ain't it?"

"Mister, you're lucky to get any place at all to sleep in this town. We've got half a dozen new silver mines in these parts producing like crazy, and there's more folks coming in all the time." The clerk looked dubiously at Longarm's rifle. "You want me to put that in the storeroom for you?"

"I reckon I'll keep it with me," said Longarm, "unless that's against the rules in a high-priced place like this."

"Naw, there ain't no ordinance against carrying guns. No ordinances of any sort, come to think of it." The clerk spun the registration book around on the desk and asked, "Well, how about it? You want the room or not?"

Longarm dropped some coins on the desk and reached for the quill pen in its holder. "I reckon," he said as he scrawled "Custis Parker, Denver, Colorado" in the book. It was an alias he used sometimes when he was keeping his real identity a secret, comprised of the first and middle names his mama had given him back in West-by-God Virginia.

The clerk slid a key across the desk. "Room Twelve, Mr. Parker," he said. "Up the stairs and all the way to the rear."

Longarm nodded his thanks and hefted his Winchester and warbag. As he carried them up the stairs, he thought that his description as the man who had provoked a fight in the Chinaman's place earlier by asking questions about Ben Mallory must not have reached the clerk. Otherwise the man would have probably been more leery of renting him a room. He wondered what the clerk would do when he eventually heard

63

the stories and realized he had a troublemaker lodging upstairs.

Until that happened, Longarm was going to get some rest.
The strain of the past few days had made him weary, and he
was feeling a little edgy from the showdown that had left the
would-be outlaw dead and J. Emerson Dupree badly
wounded. Longarm had traded lead with plenty of killers
over the course of his years as a marshal, but a fella never
got completely used to such things. As soon as he had gone
inside the hotel room and shut the door behind him, he
leaned the Winchester in a corner, put his warbag on the bed,
and fished out a well-padded bottle of Maryland rye that was
wrapped up in a pair of spare longhandled underwear. After
a long swallow, he lowered the bottle and said, ''Ahhh.''

Nothing like coming close to death for reminding a fella
that he was truly alive, thought Longarm. But that was a
feeling best experienced in small doses . . .

It was getting on toward evening when Longarm came back
downstairs. He had stretched his long frame out on the bed
and dozed for a while, but the whole time his hand had been
on the butt of the Colt he had slipped under the pillow. The
single chair that was in the room looked too rickety to be
much good for propping under the doorknob, so he had settled for leaning the Winchester against it instead. If anybody
opened the door or as much as rattled the knob, the rifle
would fall and wake him.

No one had disturbed him, though, and now he was hungry after his nap. Somehow, he didn't think the Chinaman
would want his business after what had happened there earlier in the day, and he hadn't seen a dining room downstairs
in the hotel. So Longarm shrugged into his coat and put his
hat on, prepared to go back out into the raw evening. He left
the Winchester lying on the bed as he went out. Pausing
momentarily just outside the room, he placed a match between the door and the jamb, low down so that it wouldn't
be easily noticed, then carefully shut the door. If anybody

was waiting for him inside when he got back, he'd have at least a little warning.

Judging by the look the clerk gave him, Longarm's reputation had spread to the hotel during the afternoon. The slick-haired gent frowned at Longarm and said, "You didn't tell me you came here to raise hell."

"You didn't ask," Longarm pointed out. "Anyway, my money's as good as anybody else's, ain't it?"

"There's money, and then there's money," said the clerk. "And some of it ain't worth dying over. I'd appreciate it if you'd gather your gear and leave, mister."

Longarm fired up a cheroot and said around it, "That ain't likely to happen, old son. I paid, and I'm staying. But you can tell Mallory that you did your damnedest to run me out of here. Maybe he won't hold it against you that you didn't succeed."

The clerk stared at Longarm for a moment, then said in a voice ragged with anxiety, "What the hell do you want here in Galena City, mister?"

"That's my business." Longarm blew out a cloud of smoke. "And maybe Mallory's." There. That was another prod that was bound to reach Mallory's ears sooner or later.

The clerk shook his head. He wore the look of a man staring into his own grave. "I wish you'd never come here," he said solemnly.

"Well, I'll be out of your hair for a little while," said Longarm. "Soon as you tell me where a gent could get some supper."

"Best place is the Chinaman's—" The clerk stopped short and shook his head. "No, you probably wouldn't want to go back there, would you? And even if you did, Ling wouldn't like it. Why don't you try Red Mike's, up on Comstock Street? There's already some bullet holes in Mike's walls, so a few more shouldn't make much difference."

Longarm grinned wolfishly. "Much obliged. I'll mosey on up there."

He went to the front door of the hotel, opened it, slipped

outside quickly so that he wouldn't be silhouetted against the light inside for more than an instant. According to his watch when he took it from his pocket and opened it, the hour was only five o'clock, but already night was falling. The thick clouds shut out the sun and brought on the darkness that much faster.

Every instinct Longarm possessed was on the alert as he walked up Greenwood Avenue toward Comstock Street, which formed the upper bar of the T. He was still several blocks from the intersection when a woman's voice said, "Mister? Mister, can you help me?"

The voice was wracked with pain. Longarm looked over and saw a figure leaning against the side wall of the building he was passing. His first thought was that this was some sort of trap set by Mallory, but the anguish in the woman's voice had seemed genuine. He glanced around, but he was the only one on this stretch of boardwalk, and the building was dark and closed up.

Cautiously, he stepped toward the woman. "Ma'am?" he said. "Are you all right?"

She seemed to be having trouble catching her breath, but when she moved slightly, air hissed between clenched teeth. "They . . . they dragged me back in the alley," she gasped out. "I . . . I told 'em I was a respectable woman, a married woman. They . . . they laughed at me."

Longarm saw now that she was trying to hold the tatters of a torn dress around her. He felt anger welling up inside him. "Who was it?" he asked as he stepped toward her. "Did you know them?"

"It was . . . Mallory's boys."

Longarm wasn't surprised. The outlaws thought they could get away with anything they wanted to do around here, including rape. They were sure as hell going to find out different, he vowed. He reached out to the woman. "Here, let me help you—"

"*No!*" It was a whisper, barely heard. She went on in the same low tones. "They made me say that, they threatened to kill my husband if I didn't. They saw me talking to you earlier today and figured you'd listen to me. Get out of here, mister, now!''

The words tumbled out of her, breathless and run together. But Longarm understood enough to know what she was saying. In the faint light that reached the mouth of the alley where she leaned against the wall, he recognized her as the middle-aged woman he had asked whether there was a doctor in Galena City.

Now, because of that innocent moment, she had suffered through no fault of her own, just like Dupree. Mallory's men had witnessed the conversation and decided to use her to strike back against the stranger who had come to town and started asking questions. They had beaten her, probably used her, and now she was the bait in a trap . . .

Longarm grabbed her arm. "Come on!" he barked. "Let's get out of here!"

"No!" she said again, this time crying out the word. She didn't try to pull away from Longarm, though. Instead she threw herself in front of him.

At that moment, bursts of orange fire licked out from the darkness of the alley, and gunshots shattered the silence.

The woman was thrown forward, falling against Longarm, and he caught her instinctively as he realized in horror that she had been hit by the gunfire. He saw her face, inches from his, handsome and still dignified despite the hell she had been forced to endure, and as pain twisted her features, she moaned, ''Better this way . . . after what they did to me . . .''

Then she sagged in Longarm's grip, and the rattle in her throat told him she was dead.

Guns were still blasting in the alley, and bullets sang a deadly song around Longarm's head. He felt the woman's body shudder as more slugs thudded into her back, but at least she was beyond the pain of feeling them now. Longarm reeled toward the corner of the building, intending to use it as cover if he could get there. With the woman's body in his arms, he couldn't reach his gun.

She slipped out of his grasp before he made it to the corner of the building. People on the street were yelling and running for cover as bullets chewed splinters from the planks. Longarm crouched and tried to draw his Colt, but as his fingers touched the smooth wooden grips of the weapon, something slammed into his side and twisted him around. The blow didn't hurt very much, but he was suddenly sick at his stomach. He had been shot before, and he knew the feeling.

Longarm staggered along the boardwalk. Somewhere men were running and yelling. He knew he was hurt bad, too bad to make a fight of it right now. He couldn't let Mallory's men catch him in the open. Forcing his muscles to move, he ran along the street until a dark mouth yawned to his right. He plunged into it.

This alley led past a feed store, and at the rear of the building was a tall wooden platform. Wagons could be backed up there so that heavy bags of grain could be brought from the building and loaded into them. The platform looked to be solid all around, but when Longarm paused beside it and started pulling at the boards, he found what he was looking for. Several of the boards were loose, and when he pulled them back, he formed a narrow opening into the hollow space underneath the loading platform. He went to his knees and wiggled through it, gasping as his wound was raked over the rough edge of one of the boards.

But then he was inside, in the welcoming darkness, and he tugged the boards back into place. If Mallory's men searched for him with lanterns, they would probably spot the signs of his flight and figure out where he was hidden, but there was nothing he could do about that now. His side was starting to burn as if a torch was being held to it.

Longarm was never sure how long he lay there in the mud under the loading platform, drifting in and out of consciousness. It was damned galling to have to hide from a bunch of low-down bushwhackers who had molested and then killed an innocent woman, but there was nothing else he could do right now.

He tried to keep his breathing steady for two reasons: concentrating on that helped him shut out the pain of being shot, and the less noise he made, the less likely Mallory's men were to find him. For a while, there was quite a hubbub coming from Greenwood Avenue, but then it died away. Shootings were pretty common in a place like this. As long as it didn't happen in the middle of the main street, folks just kept their heads down until the trouble was over and then went on about their business. Several times, Longarm heard men walk past the loading platform, but none of them stopped.

Finally, when enough time had passed so that he thought it might be safe to emerge, he pushed the boards aside and slithered out. He forced himself to his feet and stood there shakily while he slipped a hand under his coat and explored the wound. There was a lot of blood, and it hurt like blazes. He couldn't tell how badly he was hurt.

He needed to find that old granny woman. She could patch him up. Not wanting to draw attention to himself, he buttoned his coat over the bloodstained shirt and walked stiffly toward Greenwood Avenue. He staggered a little and knew he looked like a drunk who was making an effort not to reveal just how inebriated he really was. He reached the avenue and turned north toward Comstock. Someone would have to tell him where to find the old woman who passed for a sawbones around here, because he didn't have any idea how to locate her.

He hadn't gone more than a block before Mallory's men spotted him and started chasing him. After that, it was a matter of trying to stay ahead of them and hoping they wouldn't start shooting so that some other innocent person would be gunned down, and then he was in another alley and there was a door in front of him, and beyond the door an angel, a beautiful red-haired angel . . . She was looking down at him now, Longarm realized suddenly, and her full red lips curved in a smile. "Hello," she said. "I see you're still alive."

# Chapter 9

"I'm glad," she went on. "For a while there, we weren't sure if you were going to make it or not."

Longarm didn't say anything for a lengthy moment. Instead, he took stock of his situation. He was lying in a soft bed on what felt like clean sheets. A thick quilt was spread over him so that he was wrapped in warmth. He would have been pretty comfortable if it had not been for the tightness around his midsection and the pain that shot through him when he moved slightly.

The red-haired woman saw his grimace. "Just lie still," she told him. "You don't want that bullet wound to open up again."

She was sitting on the edge of the bed, leaning over him. The dark blue dressing gown she wore hung open enough so that he could see into it. The gap revealed much of the valley between the swells of her breasts. Her skin was fair and lightly dusted with tiny freckles. She smelled good, too, just a hint of perfume mixed with soap and clean skin. Longarm realized suddenly that she must have just come from a bath.

And he realized as well that her nearness was having an effect on him. He felt a stiffening at his groin, and as his hardness grew, he became aware that he was naked under the covers except for the bandages wrapped tightly around his middle.

"Who . . . who are you?" he managed to say. "Where am I?"

The woman shifted a little, and he saw a rosy nipple peek out of the robe for a second. "You're in my bedroom at the Silver Slipper," she said. "My name is Nola Sutton. I own this place. That was my office you barged into the other night."

"The . . . other night," repeated Longarm. "How long . . . have I . . ."

"Two days and three nights," replied Nola Sutton, knowing what he was trying to ask. "That's how long you've been unconscious. It's morning again." She stood up and walked to the window with a swish of dark blue silk. When she pulled the curtain back, brilliant sunlight slanted into the room and made Longarm wince. He narrowed his eyes against the glare. After more than forty-eight hours of darkness, he wasn't ready for that much light.

Nola Sutton strolled back over to the bed and sat down while Longarm's eyes adjusted. The window had a thin frosting of ice on it, and the frozen crystals broke the sunlight into shifting patterns of color. It probably would have been beautiful, if he had felt good enough to appreciate the sight.

He looked at her again and saw that she had drawn the robe closed. Feeling slightly disappointed, he said, "There were some fellas . . . chasing me . . ."

"Mallory's men," Nola said with a nod. "They came to my office door and knocked a few minutes after you barged in."

"You . . . didn't let 'em in?"

"I invited them to come in and look around all they wanted," she said. "By that time, I had thrown a comforter over the sofa where you were lying. They couldn't see you, and I told them that no one had been in the office all evening except me. They took my word for it and went on to look for you elsewhere."

71

"You were . . . taking a mighty big chance," Longarm told her. "If they had come in . . . and found me . . ."

"I would have killed them," Nola said simply. "My hand was on my gun in the pocket of my gown, and I know how to use it."

Longarm frowned at her. He hadn't expected such a cold-blooded answer from such a lovely woman. Evidently, she had more spunk than most of the rest of the people in town combined.

"I thought Mallory . . . had everybody in Galena City buffaloed," he said.

Nola shook her head. "Not everyone is afraid of him, and he knows it. His men have their orders. They know not to push me too far."

"Well, I'm obliged for what you've done for me."

She smiled and shrugged. "I've always had a soft spot in my heart for strays."

"You reckon that's what I am?" asked Longarm, returning her smile.

"You certainly looked like you'd had better days. After Mallory's men were gone, I had you brought up here and sent one of my girls for Granny Winslow. When she saw how much blood you'd lost, she told me you'd probably die. I told her to do her best for you. Now that you're awake, I'm convinced that you're going to live after all. I can tell by your eyes that you're a very stubborn man."

"I'll take that . . . as a compliment," murmured Longarm. "Right now I'm . . . a mighty sleepy man all of a sudden."

"Then you should rest," Nola said softly. "When you wake up again, you should eat something, but for now, just sleep."

That sounded good to Longarm. He closed his eyes and allowed himself to drift away. As sleep began to claim him, though, he suddenly asked himself a question: now that Nola Sutton had him, what was she going to do with him?

He dozed off before he could come up with an answer.

•   •   •

72

True to her word, Nola had a bowl of hot broth waiting for him when he woke up again. Only she didn't deliver it herself. Instead, when Longarm opened his eyes, he found a young woman with blond hair bending over the bed. "Are you awake?" she asked brightly.

"I reckon I am," Longarm replied. He shifted and found that the pain in his side, while still there, was not as sharp this time. It didn't take his breath away.

But the blond damned near did. She was big—tall, broad-shouldered, heavy-breasted. She looked like the sort of girl who had been raised on a farm or a ranch, and fairly recently, too, since she wasn't more than twenty years old. Her skin even retained a trace of a tan that working in the sun must have given her. At the moment, however, her working outfit was considerably different than it had probably been earlier in her life. She was wearing a short red dress with a flouncy skirt and black lace stockings. The dress was cut low enough to reveal the upper third of her large breasts. Thick wings of hair a shade lighter than honey framed her lovely face and fell past her shoulders.

"I have some broth here that the cook just brought up," she said to Longarm. "I want you to eat every bit of it."

"Yes, ma'am," he said. He wasn't in the habit of arguing with ladies as pretty as she was, and besides, in his weakened condition, she could hold him down and spoon-feed him if she was of a mind to.

She helped him sit up in bed, propping several pillows behind him. The quilt slipped, and Longarm grabbed for it out of habit. The blond laughed and said, "Don't mind about that, honey. There's nothing under those covers I haven't seen plenty of times before."

"That may be true in general, ma'am," said Longarm, "but you ain't seen this particular one."

She laughed again. "Don't be too sure. Somebody had to get those bloody clothes off of you and help clean you up, you know." She gave him a mischievous smile. "I've been looking forward to getting to know you better when you

73

aren't passed out from a gunshot wound. By the way, my name's Angie.''

She stuck out her hand like a man, and Longarm shook with her. "You can call me Custis," he said.

"I know. Your name's Custis Parker. Nola heard some of the men talking about you. You rode into town, raised hell, and got shot, all in one day." Angie suddenly frowned. "Some people say you killed Mrs. Keegan. Is that true?"

"Is that the woman who was shot in the back in an alley?" Longarm suddenly felt even worse about the woman's death. He hadn't even known her name when she had saved his life and lost her own in the process.

"She was shot, all right, and she'd been abused." Angie was glaring at him now.

Longarm met her gaze squarely and said, "I didn't kill the lady, Angie. I was there, but it was the men who were trying to bushwhack me who shot her. They're the ones who abused her, too, and then sent her to try to trap me."

She nodded, and Longarm could tell she believed him without reservation, now that she had heard it from his own lips. She said, "They were Mallory's men, weren't they?"

"I reckon so." Longarm sighed. "I suppose when you get right down to it, I *am* to blame for Mrs. Keegan's death. I was trying to stir things up by asking questions about Mallory. I guess I stirred them up a little too good."

"I think I'd be better off if I didn't hear about all that," said Angie. She went to a dresser on the other side of the room. A tray with a bowl on it sat there, and Longarm saw wisps of steam rising from the bowl. He could smell a delicious aroma in the air, too, and the realization hit him suddenly that it had been a long time since he'd had anything to eat. Hard on the heels of that thought came his stomach, cramping with hunger.

Angie brought the tray over to the bed. "Can you manage by yourself, or do you want me to feed you?"

"I'm a mite light-headed, but I'll give it a try." Longarm reached for the spoon beside the bowl.

Before he could reach it, a wave of dizziness hit him, and he had to sag back against the pillows. Angie said firmly, "You just sit there, Custis. I'll take care of you."

"I reckon I'd better let you," he said reluctantly. "I wouldn't want to spill that broth."

"Absolutely not. It's hot, and if you dump it in your lap, you might burn something important."

Longarm chuckled. She was a brazen hussy, he thought, but what else could you expect from a gal who worked in a saloon? That didn't mean he was going to like her any less. Some of the best women he'd ever known had been the ones whom society found the least respectable.

She spooned up some of the broth and leaned toward him, saying, "Open wide." Longarm took the spoon in his mouth and swallowed the hot broth, and as he did so, he noticed that Angie was holding her own mouth open slightly, and her tongue darted out to lick over her lips. She was breathing a little harder, too, he realized as she continued to feed him. Obviously, it didn't take a whole hell of a lot to get her all hot and bothered. Right about now, Longarm could say the same thing about himself.

All in all, it was a mighty interesting meal, but Longarm was still too weak to do anything about it. He ate as much of the broth as he could and then lay back down again, letting the strength from the broth seep into him. He felt himself growing drowsy again and didn't fight the sensation. The last thing he was aware of was Angie bending over him and pressing her lips to his forehead. "Sleep well, Custis," she whispered.

Longarm tried not to lose all track of time. The curtains had been closed when Angie was in the room with him, and he had assumed it was night again. They were still closed when he awoke, but he saw strips of brightness around them that told him it was day once more.

He was aware of something else—a pressing need in his bladder. He lay there for a moment, trying to ignore it, but that was impossible. With a groan, he pushed the covers back and started to swing his legs out of bed.

"Here now! What do you think you're doing?" a woman's voice asked him sharply.

Longarm froze. He was uncovered, and his manhood was standing up straight and tall, not from arousal but from the need to relieve himself. Whatever the reason, it was enough to draw the attention of the woman who was standing up from a chair on the other side of the room.

Coolly, she appraised his shaft, then shifted her gaze to his face as if she wasn't overly impressed. "You shouldn't be getting out of bed," she said. "If you need something, I'll get it for you."

She was a brunette, slender in a simple gray dress. Longarm put her age somewhere between Nola Sutton and Angie. She was pretty, too. Not as elegantly lovely as Nola or as earthily attractive as Angie, but definitely pretty in a dark, intense way. Under other circumstances, Longarm was sure he would have appreciated her looks even more, but right now he had other things on his mind.

"Chamber pot," he grated out.

The woman nodded. "I'll fetch it for you." She went to the end of the bed and bent down to pick up a porcelain pot with a handle on it. She carried it around to Longarm.

He practically grabbed it out of her hands. "Much obliged," he said. When she didn't go anywhere, he added, "That's all. I reckon you can go now, ma'am."

She shook her head and said, "I don't think so. I don't want you falling and injuring yourself again, Mr. Parker. Nola would never forgive me."

Longarm thought there was a slight accent to her words, but he didn't take the time to ponder the question of where she was from. "Ma'am," he said through gritted teeth, "if you'll just step out of the room . . ."

"I'll turn my back and go over there," she said, pointing to the far side of the room.

Longarm hesitated, then nodded in agreement. A little em-

76

barrassment was one thing; having his bladder blow up was another.

When he was finished, he leaned over and put the chamber pot back under the bed himself, knowing that if he didn't, the brunette would do so. Bending hurt his side, but it wasn't anything he couldn't stand. He sat back in the bed and pulled the covers over himself again. "Much obliged," he repeated.

The brunette turned. "I'm called Rafaela," she said. "If there's anything you need . . ."

Longarm was hungry again, but this time he wanted more than broth. "I reckon I could do with some solid food," he said.

Rafaela nodded. "All right. The cook should have something left over from breakfast. I'll see what I can find—but only if you promise to stay in bed."

"Yes, ma'am. I'm feeling a mite stronger than I was, but I don't reckon I'm up to dancing a jig just yet."

Rafaela smiled faintly and turned toward the door. She paused and looked back at him. "Just one more thing, Mr. Parker," she said. "Don't call me ma'am. I'm a whore, not a schoolteacher."

The undertone of bitterness in her voice took him by surprise. Angie certainly hadn't seemed bothered by what she did for a living. Rafaela was obviously different, though.

Longarm shook his head and said, "I can't help it, ma'am. My ma raised me to respect women no matter what. I'm too old to be breaking any habits now, Miss Rafaela."

She caught her breath, and Longarm thought he saw a flash of something in her eyes, maybe a chink in the cool facade she put up. But then she said, "I don't suppose it matters, does it?"

Before he could answer, she was gone.

When the door opened a few minutes later, he expected to see Rafaela coming back with his food. Instead, yet another young woman brought the tray into the room. She smiled at Longarm, seemingly totally unmindful of the fact that she wore only a thin shift that clearly outlined her small breasts and long, sensuous legs. Straight hair the color of midnight hung far down her back, almost to the curve of her hips. She was Chinese, and her face possessed a doll-like prettiness. She was definitely flesh and blood, though, and so was Longarm. He became all too aware of that as his eyes lingered on the dark, erect nipples thrusting out against the gauzy material of the shift.

"Good Lord!" he exclaimed. "How many of you gals *are* there?"

She looked confused by the question, and he wondered how much English she spoke, if any. She could speak the lingo at least a little, he discovered, because she said, "I am called Mickey. Rafaela say to bring you this food."

The tray in her hands contained a plate filled with steak, potatoes, gravy, and biscuits. Longarm practically snatched it out of her hands as she brought it over to the bed. He didn't know what looked better to him right now—the food or the woman. He was glad he didn't have to decide between them.

He dug in with the knife and fork on the tray as Mickey went over to a chair and primly sat down. "I wait, take back tray," she said.

"That'll be fine," Longarm told her. He kept eating.

Despite his hunger, his eyes kept straying over to her. In her own way, she was as attractive as Nola and Angie and Rafaela, and just as different as each of them, too. Even dressed as provocatively as she was, there was an innocence about her, a quality that was almost childlike, although she was definitely not a child.

Fate had a damned peculiar sense of humor, he thought. Here he was being attended to by all manner of beautiful women, and although he had responded physically to all of them, there wasn't a thing he could do about it right now. His strength might be coming back, and the bullet hole in his side might be healing, but he would still have to recover quite a bit before he could properly bed any woman again, let alone beauties like his four nursemaids.

And to be honest, none of the four ladies had even expressed an interest in crawling into bed with him except for Angie, he reminded himself.

He was just mopping up the last of the gravy with the final bite of biscuit when the door opened and Nola Sutton came into the room. She was wearing a green dress that was provocative without being brazen. She smiled and said, "Hello, Mr. Parker. How are you feeling?"

Longarm swallowed the last bite and said honestly, "A whole heap better. I could do with a pot of coffee, though."

Nola nodded. "I'll see that one is brought up." She turned her head and spoke to the Chinese girl. "Mickey, take Mr. Parker's tray downstairs and then bring him some coffee."

Mickey stood. "Yes, Miss Nola." She kept her eyes downcast.

Nola put her hand under Mickey's chin and gently tipped her head up so that the young woman had no choice but to look at her. "You're not in China any longer," Nola reminded her. "You may work for me, but you're not a slave, Mickey."

Mickey smiled. "I will try to remember."

When Mickey was gone, Longarm commented to Nola, "That's, ah, an unusual gal."

"Not so unusual," said Nola. "She came over here as a child with the rest of her family. Her father and brothers helped build the Central Pacific Railroad. There wasn't enough money to feed everyone in the family, though, so when Mickey was seven, her father sold her."

Longarm's jaw tightened. "That's a hell of a thing to do."

"I agree. That's why I bought her from the man who owned her when he came through here a while back."

"You bought her," repeated Longarm.

"It was the only way to get her away from him. Just another business transaction, as far as he was concerned." For a moment, a faraway look appeared on Nola's face. "But it

79

wasn't just business any longer when Mickey told me some of the things he'd done to her. A couple of the men who work for me caught up to the son of a bitch between here and Virginia City and brought him back. I explained to him why he was going to die before I—''

She stopped short and took a deep breath, then went on. ''But I shouldn't be telling these things to a lawman, should I? Even though you're a federal man, and murder is a state crime.''

Longarm tensed, and his mind flashed back to the night he had blundered into Nola's office with a bullet hole in his side. He remembered her saying something then about him being a marshal. Obviously, she had found his badge and bona fides.

''Who else knows?'' he asked grimly.

''That you're a lawman?'' Nola shook her head. ''Only me. I didn't tell any of the girls. And only Rafaela, Angie, Mickey, and the cook know you're up here. I've asked them not to say anything to anyone, and I can trust them.''

''You're sure about that?''

''Certain. I'd trust any of them with my life.''

''That's just what you're doing,'' said Longarm, ''by hiding me out from Mallory.''

''I told you before, I'm not frightened of Mallory—''

That was when a gun went off downstairs.

# Chapter 10

Longarm and Nola both stiffened in surprise. He sat up straighter in the bed while she turned toward the door. "Wait a minute," Longarm said sharply as he prepared to throw the covers back and swing his legs out of bed. "I'll help—"

Nola thrust a hand toward him, palm out. "You stay right there!" she ordered. "Whatever's going on down there, I'll handle it. You don't have to worry about me."

There had been only the single gunshot, but Longarm didn't know whether that was good or bad. He wanted to get out of the bed and go see what was happening, but he knew Nola was right. He was still in no shape for trouble, and besides, he didn't even know where his pants were.

He would have looked a sight, showing up at the top of the stairs naked as a jaybird except for the bandage around his midsection. People might have stopped what they were doing just to gawk at him, though, he thought dryly.

"Go on," he said to Nola. "I'll be right here if you need me. Just be careful."

"I always am," she told him. "That's how I've stayed alive."

He could believe that. No woman ran a place like the Silver Slipper without being able to take care of herself.

• • •

Nola slipped her hand into the cleverly concealed pocket of her dress as she left the room and started along the balcony toward the stairs. Her pistol was there, loaded and ready to use. As she approached the top of the broad staircase, she heard loud, angry voices coming from below.

She paused at the head of the stairs and looked down at the big main room of the Silver Slipper spread out below her. It was brightly lit by gas chandeliers, the only such fixtures in Galena City. Like the huge mirrors behind the long mahogany bar, the bar itself, the gaming tables covered with green baize, the embossed wallpaper, and all the other ornate furnishings, the chandeliers had cost her a pretty penny. It was a fact of the saloon business, though, that customers tended to spend more when a place looked like the owner didn't really need the money. Illusion was what really mattered the most.

Just like the most important thing about being a whore was making the customer believe that he was different from all the other men who had shared your bed . . .

Nola put that thought out of her head and concentrated on the matter at hand. She saw a knot of men at the far end of the bar, near the front windows. Half a dozen of them wore silk vests and sleeve garters over spotless white shirts, and she identified them as her bartenders. They were surrounding four men in range clothes. One of the cowboys was bareheaded and was rubbing his jaw as if he had just been punched. That was probably what had happened, Nola decided, because his hat was on the floor at his feet where it would have fallen when it was knocked off his head.

Everyone else in the room was looking at the group at the end of the bar. Gambling had ceased, and so had drinking and laughing and fondling the gaudily clad young women who worked for Nola. That meant the money had stopped flowing for the moment, as well, and she couldn't have that, Nola thought.

"What's going on here?" she said as she started down

the stairs, her voice not overly loud but still ringing clearly throughout the room. Plenty of eyes turned to look at her as she descended the staircase, and she enjoyed the attention.

One of the bartenders who had surrounded the cowboys swung around to face her as she approached. "Sorry for the disturbance, Miss Nola," he said. "One of these gents got a little rowdy and decided to take a potshot at the chandeliers. We took the gun away from him before he could do any real harm."

"Them sons o' bitches jumped me for no good reason at all!" blustered the cowboy. "I wasn't goin' to really hurt anything."

Nola's man moved aside so that she got her first good look at the troublemaker and his companions. She tensed as she saw that they weren't simple cowhands after all.

They were some of Ben Mallory's men.

Nola had already been in Galena City and the Silver Slipper had been well established when Mallory's gang had shown up a couple of months earlier and proceeded to run roughshod over the entire town. They had left the Silver Slipper alone for the most part because Mallory himself had sauntered in that first night, seen Nola, and decided that he wanted her. As soon as she had seen the raw wanting in his eyes, she had known that he had no real power over her. It was the other way around, in fact. And letting Mallory bed her was a small price to pay to protect her investment, as far as she was concerned. Ever since then, the outlaws had pretty much steered clear of the Silver Slipper, and when they did come in here, they usually behaved themselves.

Tonight, though, these men must have gotten drunk somewhere else before coming here. Otherwise, they wouldn't have been so belligerent.

Nola told herself to stay calm. She could handle this problem. With a smile, she said, "I think you boys have probably had enough celebrating for one night. Why don't you come back again some other time?"

"What about my gun?" the bareheaded outlaw demanded,

83

pointing to the revolver being held by one of the bartenders.

"You can drop by any time tomorrow and pick it up," Nola told him.

The man shook his head. "I want it back now," he said stubbornly.

It wasn't worth arguing over, Nola decided after a moment's thought. The man certainly wasn't going to try to cause any more trouble, not when he and his friends were surrounded by Nola's bartenders, all of whom were large and tough. She nodded to the one with the gun and said, "Give it back to him." To the outlaw, she added, "But you'll have to leave now."

The man snatched his gun out of the bartender's hand. "Soon as I'm damned good and ready," he snarled. "You can't treat Ben Mallory's boys like shit!"

He spun around, jerked the gun up, and started pulling the trigger.

Men dove out of the way of the shots, but the outlaw wasn't really directing the bullets at anyone in particular. Instead, he was firing at the shelves of the backbar, where dozens of bottles of liquor stood under the big mirrors. Bottles shattered in a shower of glass splinters and whiskey. Several of Nola's men gathered themselves to leap at the crazed outlaw, but Nola stopped them by shouting, "No!" If her men jumped him, he might turn and kill one of them.

Instead, she slipped the pistol from her pocket and shot him in the back.

The other outlaws grabbed for their guns as Nola's bullet drove the man against the bar. Before they could draw their weapons, however, the bartenders lunged at them. A couple of the outlaws went down under hard-fisted blows, while the final one was laid out by a chair that was busted over his head. The melee was over almost before it had a chance to get started.

The man Nola had shot had dropped his gun and was clawing at the bar in an effort to hold himself up. He slid down to the sawdust-littered floor, moaning in pain. Nola had shot him high on the left side, possibly breaking his shoulder blade but not doing any more damage than that.

"Your friend will live," Nola said coldly to the other outlaws when they had been disarmed. "Get him out of here, and don't come back."

"You can't throw us out!" said one of the men. "Don't you know who we are?"

Nola lifted her pistol and eared back the hammer as she pointed it at the bridge of the man's nose. The gun was a small caliber, but from that angle, the barrel must have looked as big around as a cannon. "It doesn't matter who you are," Nola told him. "If you don't do what I told you, in another minute you'll just be one more dead son of a bitch."

The outlaw paled, swallowed hard, and jerked his head toward the door. "Grab hold of Brewster there," he told his companions. "Let's get out of here. We ain't stayin' where we ain't wanted!"

"I suppose that eliminates practically the entire world, then," murmured Nola.

The outlaws didn't seem to have heard the acerbic comment. They gathered up their fallen comrade and half carried, half dragged him out of the saloon. Nola put her gun away and turned to the other customers with a brilliant smile. "That concludes our little impromptu entertainment," she said. "Now you good people can go back to enjoying your evening."

All eyes were still on her as she crossed the room and went back up the stairs. The music, the laughter, and the talking didn't really get under way again until she was gone, but by the time she reached the door of Longarm's room, everything sounded like it was back to normal.

Longarm's hands had clenched into fists when he heard the rattle of gunfire downstairs erupt once more. He was afraid for Nola, afraid that somehow Ben Mallory had found out he was here and had come to take revenge on Nola for helping him. He threw back the covers and stood up, moving stiffly, then hobbled toward a tall wardrobe on the other side of the room next to the dressing table. Sure enough, when he opened the door of the wardrobe, he found his clothes hanging in there. The shirt still had a bullet hole in the front and back, but the blood had been washed out of it as much as possible, leaving only a faint stain.

At the moment, he was more interested in retrieving his pants—and the gunbelt that was hanging on a peg on the side of the chifforobe.

He took the pants down and stepped into them carefully. A wave of dizziness hit him while he had one foot off the floor, and he almost fell. He would have if he hadn't reached out quickly and grabbed the chifforobe door. When he felt steadier, he finished pulling on his pants and then reached for the gun. He had just slipped the Colt out of the holster and turned toward the door of Nola's bedroom when it opened.

"What are you doing out of bed?" she demanded as she stepped into the room and closed the door behind her.

"I heard more shots," Longarm said gruffly. "Figured I'd better get ready for trouble."

"It was nothing I couldn't handle," she said. "Now put that gun away, take those pants off, and get back into bed."

"What happened?" demanded Longarm, ignoring her orders.

"Some of Mallory's men decided to raise a little hell," she said offhandedly. "One of them shot a few bottles of whiskey, but that was all the damage. I shot him before he could hurt anything else."

"You shot him," repeated Longarm with a frown.

"I just wounded him."

It was starting to look like Nola Sutton was a dangerous woman. She had practically admitted that she had killed the man who had abused Mickey, and now she talked about shooting a troublemaking owlhoot like it was nothing more than swatting a fly. Maybe he had better do what she told him, he thought, before she took a gun to him.

But he had a stubborn streak, so he said, "I've been lying in that bed for quite a while now. Feels pretty good to be up and about."

"It'll feel even better when you've got more of your strength back." She came closer to him and tipped her head back so that she could look at his face as she laid a hand on his bare chest. "I'll bet you don't often refuse when a lady asks you to take your clothes off and get into her bed."

"That's because she's usually planning on shedding her duds and getting into bed, too," he said.

That brought a smile and a laugh from her. Her hands went to the buttons of his trousers. "I suppose that can be arranged. But you first."

Longarm let her unfasten the buttons and push the trousers down around his bare ankles. He stepped out of them, and as he did, his stiffening manhood bobbed near her hand. She reached out, as natural as could be, and closed her fingers warmly around the thick pole of male flesh.

She massaged him sensuously, and the idea of standing there practically naked while she was fully dressed and caressing him finished bringing him to full arousal. Considering how weak he still was, his shaft throbbed with surprising strength.

"You promised you'd lie down," whispered Nola.

Longarm's voice was husky as he replied, "You promised you'd take your clothes off and join me."

"All in good time." She leaned over, and her lips trailed kisses across his chest, moving from nipple to nipple through the thick mat of brown hair.

Longarm let her steer him over to the bed. He lay back and watched with great pleasure as she slowly stripped for him. Each layer of clothing that came off and joined the pile on the floor revealed more of her body, until finally she slid a silky shift down over her hips and stepped out of it to stand before him, fully, resplendently nude. Her skin was creamy and dotted with an occasional freckle, and her fairness made

87

the triangle of fine-spun auburn hair between her legs seem that much darker. Her breasts rode high and proud on her chest, each of them crowned with a dark red nipple.

"You're going to have to let me do all the work," she told him as she approached the bed. "I don't want you exerting yourself."

Longarm began, "I ain't in the habit of just lying back—"

"That's what you're going to do this time," Nola said firmly. She sat down on the bed beside Longarm and reached over to grasp him.

The groan that came from his throat was one of pleasure, not pain, as her hand enfolded his shaft and began to slowly pump it. Her touch was expert, and he tried not to think about all the other men she had doubtless held this way. Sliding, gliding up and down along the pole of flesh, her fingers quickly brought him to a fever-pitch.

Just when he thought he was about to spend himself in her hand, she stopped and gripped him tightly around the base of the stalk for a moment. Then she leaned over farther, cupped her right breast in her hand, and used the hard, pebbled nipple to tease the slit at the head of his shaft. Again Longarm groaned.

All his instincts told him to grab her, roll her onto her back, and plant himself inside her. With an effort, he controlled that urge and let her continue working her magic on him. She knelt above him and pressed her breasts together, trapping his manhood between the soft globes in an embrace that was searing. He was practically trembling now with the need for release.

She sat up, straddling his legs, and began to massage his strong, muscular thighs. Occasionally one hand would stray to gently fondle the sac that hung just below his manhood. She bent over and nuzzled the sac with her lips, then parted them and drew first one and then the other orb into her mouth. Her other hand lifted his leg slightly so that her fingers could dig into the muscles that lay along the back of his thigh.

Longarm's pulse was hammering like thunder in his head by the time she finally shifted again and her lips closed over the head of his shaft. Her tongue darted around it, tracing wet circles that burned like fire. Her hand wrapped around the lower part of the shaft and began pumping again as she sucked. With his chest rising and falling as if he had just run a mile, Longarm reached out and tangled his fingers in her thick red hair, cupping the back of her head as she bobbed up and down above him. She took him deeper and deeper into the hot, wet cavern of her mouth.

Longarm knew he couldn't stand that sort of exquisite torment for very long, and sure enough, a few moments later he felt his climax beginning to boil up. He let go of Nola's head in case she wanted to pull away, but instead she engulfed him even more. Her hips were thrusting back and forth now, and he knew that what she was doing to him was equally arousing to her. She reached underneath him and tightly gripped the cheeks of his ass as his seed began to pour out of him in scalding jets. Despite his efforts to remain still, Longarm's back arched up off the bed.

His climax seemed to last forever, spasm after spasm that totally drained him. Nola took it all, and she shook wildly as her own culmination gripped her.

Finally, Longarm fell back, spent. Nola sagged against him, equally satiated. His softening manhood was still in her mouth, and she squeezed the last drops from it, lapping up his juices like a kitten with cream. Then she licked him clean, up and down, and gave him one a final squeeze.

She slid up alongside him on the bed and after a moment was able to ask breathlessly, "Are you all right?"

"Yep," said Longarm, just as breathless as she was. "I reckon I am."

Gingerly, she explored the bandages around his middle. "We don't seem to have broken that wound open again. I'd hate to think that what we just did might wind up killing you."

Longarm put his arm around her and drew her close

89

against him. The clean scent of her hair filled his senses. "I reckon there are a whole lot worse ways for a fella to die," he said.

"Yes, but I'm not through with you, Custis. Not by a long shot."

And just what, wondered Longarm, did she mean by *that*?

He didn't have long to ponder the question, because he fell asleep like that, with Nola wrapped snugly in his arms.

# Chapter 11

Longarm had been told more than once by various sawbones who had patched him up that he had the constitution of an ox. Over the next couple of days, that quality demonstrated itself once again. Strength flowed back into his body, and the stiffness and soreness in his side where the bullet had ventilated him began to ease. He wasn't ready to hop on the back of a bucking bronc, but he was sure starting to feel more like himself again.

Nola had a lot to do with that, he knew. She watched over him like a hawk, making sure that he got plenty to eat and plenty of rest, too. And if she wasn't around to tend to his every need, then Angie or Rafaela or Mickey were there with him. He could dress himself without too much trouble now, so he got up several times a day and walked around the room to keep his muscles limber.

A couple of times a day, Nola made sure that one muscle in particular stayed good and limber. Longarm still had to lie on his back while she rode him, but that was all right—for now. Sooner or later, though, he vowed, he was going to climb on top of her and show her what he could do when he really got to going.

Angie would have been glad to take over that duty from Nola, Longarm suspected, but the big blond always stopped at just flirting with him. He had a feeling that Nola had given Angie orders not to carry her nursemaiding too far.

By the morning of the third day after the trouble downstairs, Longarm was getting edgy. He had come to Galena City to find Ben Mallory and put a stop to the silver robberies, after all, and he was no closer to that now than when he had ridden into the settlement. His mood grew even more tense when Mickey brought in his breakfast and he found a copy of this week's Galena City *Bugle* lying next to his plate. The newspaper was folded, but Longarm could read several of the headlines. One of them announced, *Stagecoach Robbery—Another Atrocity Committed—Killers at Large*.

He snatched up the paper so violently that Mickey gasped in surprise and stepped back. He glanced up at her and muttered, "Sorry." Then he returned his attention to the newspaper article that had caught his eye.

The story was bylined J. Emerson Dupree, as were several other articles on the front page, including one whose headline read *Crusading Editor Vilely Assaulted*. Dupree had recovered enough to write the story of his own wounding at the hands of the bushwhacker who had been trying to kill Longarm. The lawman was glad to know that Dupree was evidently all right.

He read the story of the latest stagecoach robbery first. Two days earlier, a coach from Bat Thompson's California & Nevada line had been stopped by bandits between Rawhide and Carson City. The outlaws had stolen the mailbags and looted the valuables from the passengers, and when one of them, a drummer named Clancy, had been too slow to turn over his watch, one of the bandits had brutally gunned him down. The killer was rumored to be none other than Ben Mallory, the reputed leader of the gang.

Longarm frowned when he read that. Dupree was liable to get in trouble with Mallory by printing such accusations in his newspaper. On the other hand, Mallory might be the sort who enjoyed the notoriety. A surprising number of badmen didn't care what was written about them, as long as their names were spelled right. A lot of outlaws had that in common with politicians, among other things, reflected Longarm.

Mickey broke into his reverie by asking, "You not like breakfast?"

Longarm looked up and realized he hadn't touched the food or the coffee Mickey had brought to him. "It's fine," he told her. "I was just looking at something here in the paper."

He forced himself to put the *Bugle* aside and eat some of the scrambled eggs and sausage and biscuits. He washed it down with several sips of black coffee and wished he had his bottle of Maryland rye. A dollop or two of it would go mighty good in the coffee.

Well, you're in the biggest saloon in town, old son, he told himself. They probably had a bottle of Tom Moore downstairs. He asked Mickey about it, and she nodded with an eager smile. "I go fetch," she said, and hurried out of the room.

That gave Longarm a chance to look at the newspaper again without offending her. He read the rest of the story about the stagecoach holdup without really learning anything more, then scanned the article concerning Dupree's shooting. According to Dupree's story, he had been accidentally wounded when he got caught in a fracas between a local miner and an unknown visitor to Galena City. The stranger had killed the miner and then dropped out of sight.

There was no mention of Ben Mallory in this story, and that was just fine with Longarm. Mallory had to be wondering what had happened to the mysterious stranger who had ridden into town, asked some questions, killed a man, been wounded, then disappeared.

Let him wonder. That would help keep him off balance until Longarm was ready to make a move again—although it didn't seem to have stopped him from continuing his murderous reign of terror along the stagecoach route.

With a sigh, Longarm put the paper aside. He wondered

if the drummer who had been murdered in the latest holdup had been one of the men who had ridden the stagecoach with him before. Too many people had died or been hurt in this case: Amelia Loftus, Mrs. Keegan, even J. Emerson Dupree. All of them had suffered because of Ben Mallory's greed.

He was going to take particular pleasure in seeing Mallory brought to justice.

Nola had her ledgers spread out on one of the poker tables downstairs. She was sitting in a corner, out of the way. At this time of day, the Silver Slipper didn't have as many customers, but the place was still fairly busy. Nola enjoyed listening to the buzz of conversation, the clink of bottle on glass, the whisper of pasteboards being shuffled and dealt, as she worked on her books.

Mickey came down the stairs and went behind the bar. That caught Nola's eye. The young Chinese woman was supposed to take breakfast up to their special guest this morning, and here she was rummaging around behind the bar. Nola's lips tightened as she stood up. She would have to have a talk with Mickey.

She was waiting at the end of the bar when Mickey came back with a bottle of Maryland rye in her hands. Instantly, Nola figured out what she was doing, and she had a twinge of guilt over the flash of anger she'd felt toward Mickey. She nodded at the bottle and asked in a low voice that only Mickey could hear, "Is that for our guest?"

"He want," replied Mickey with a nod. "I say I bring to him." Suddenly, she looked worried. "I do wrong?"

Nola smiled and shook her head. "No, not at all." She reached for the bottle of rye. "I'll take it up to him, though."

Before she could take the bottle from Mickey, the doors opened loudly and made Nola look around. A cold wind whipped into the room, and with it came three men. Nola recognized them instantly. Two of them had been in the bunch she had kicked out of the saloon a few nights earlier.

The third man, the one in the lead, was Ben Mallory.

He was tall and slender, but his build was deceptive. Nola had felt for herself the strength in his ropy muscles. He wore a hip-length coat open over a black-and-white cowhide vest. A bright red scarf was knotted around his neck, and his hat was cocked back jauntily on his black curly hair. He was grinning, as usual, but the expression did little to disguise the cruelty in his eyes. When his gaze found her standing at the end of the bar, he called loudly, "Nola! How you doin', beautiful?"

She greeted him with a nod and said coolly, "Ben. How are you?"

"Why, I'm just fine, just fine and dandy." He always sounded as if he was on the verge of breaking into delighted laughter. She could tell he wasn't as amused as he sounded, though. His jaw was taut, and anger glittered in his eyes.

Maybe she could head off this trouble. With a smile of her own, she asked, "How about a drink? It's on the house."

"All right," he agreed. "That's mighty nice of you. Yes, ma'am, mighty hospitable."

Nola turned toward Mickey and motioned for her to take the bottle and go on. She hoped mightily that Custis stayed upstairs and didn't find out Mallory was down here. She wasn't sure what connection there was between the two men, only that it involved the law somehow, and in her line of work, she had learned not to ask too many questions. But obviously there was bad blood between the two men, otherwise Mallory's gunnies wouldn't have put a bullet through Custis and then chased him into her office.

One of the bartenders had a bottle and a glass ready for her when she reached for them. As she was pouring the drink for Mallory, she said, "I always try to be hospitable, Ben, you know that."

"Well, I always thought so," said Mallory. He took the glass of whiskey she handed to him. While he lifted it to his lips and drained it with one swift backward tilt of his head, Nola signaled to the bartender to pour drinks for Mallory's men, too. Mallory lowered his glass, licked his lips, and said,

"Ahhh." He set the glass on the bar. "Mighty nice, Nola. But I hear you weren't so nice to some of my boys the other night. In fact, I hear you shot Brewster in the back."

His tone was mild, and he still sounded as if he wanted to chuckle. Nola knew that meant he was even more dangerous than usual. She tried not to let him see how nervous she was as she said, "He was shooting up my place. He was liable to kill one of my customers. I couldn't have that, so I stopped him."

"By shooting him?" Mallory prodded with a sly smile.

Suddenly, she couldn't take any more of his smug arrogance. "Yes, by shooting him," she snapped. "But I didn't kill him, and I could have."

"No, Brewster ain't dead," agreed Mallory, "but he's no good to me anymore, either. His shoulder's smashed, and he may never heal up so that he can ride and shoot like he used to."

Nola shrugged. "That's a shame. But I didn't make him get liquored up and start raising hell in my place."

"Now, Nola," said Mallory in a gently chiding voice, "you wouldn't even have a place if it wasn't for me, and you know it."

"That's not true," she said. "The Silver Slipper is mine."

"And Galena City is mine." His bantering tone finally dropped away as he went on. "The only reason you have this saloon is because I let you keep it."

Nola took a deep breath. She had nearly let this situation get out of control, and she had to stop things from getting worse. She smiled again and put her hand on Mallory's arm, moving closer to him as she said, "Now, Ben, there's no need to get upset. Why don't we go upstairs and talk about this?"

Even as she posed the question, she knew that she would have to take him to one of the other rooms. Her own bedroom was occupied at the moment—by the man Mallory evidently wanted dead. But that was all right, she could come up with some excuse Mallory would accept for the change in rooms—

"I don't think so," Mallory said coldly.

Nola blinked in surprise. "What?"

"I ain't goin' to let you and your honeypot talk me out of doin' what's right, Nola. I can't let you get away with what you did. If I was to do that, some of the other piss-poor excuses for citizens in this town might start to get ideas."

"Ben, you can't—"

"I can do anything I damn well want to," he snarled.

Then he backhanded her savagely across the face.

The blow rocked Nola's head sharply to the side and made rockets explode behind her eyes. She staggered and might have fallen if Mallory had not grabbed her arm and jerked her cruelly toward him. He slapped her again, once, twice. The pain and the shock robbed Nola of her senses. Mallory shoved her roughly against the bar. The impact knocked the wind out of her.

As she held on to the bar to keep from falling, she saw that several of the Silver Slipper's patrons had jumped to their feet in outrage. But Mallory's men had drawn their guns, one of them covering the bartenders, the other menacing the customers spread around the room. Nola gasped for breath and called out, "No! No, it . . . it's all right." She motioned weakly for the bartenders to back off and for everyone else to sit down.

No one was going to die in here today, not if she could do anything to prevent it.

Mallory had that maddening grin on his face again. "I'm sorry I had to do that, Nola," he said, but he didn't sound sorry at all to her. "Reckon I had to teach you a lesson, though. You ought to know by now who really runs things around here, and just because I enjoy beddin' you now and then, that don't make no difference. You understand?"

She understood, all right.

When she didn't say anything, he reached out and took hold of her chin, roughly jerking her head up. "I said, do you—"

"I understand," she hissed at him through gritted teeth. Her jaw ached like blazes where he had hit her, and she could feel her face beginning to puff up already. The bruises would begin to show before long.

"Good," he said, and then, unbelievably, he leaned over and kissed her on the forehead. "Just because I had to teach you a lesson don't mean I don't still love you."

The son of a bitch. The complete, utter son of a bitch. She hoped that what passed for his soul would rot in hell for a thousand eternities.

But she managed to smile a little through the pain and nodded as she said, "I know."

Mallory turned toward the bar. He gestured toward his men and said, "You can put them guns away now, boys. Nobody's goin' to cause any trouble in here. We're just as welcome as we can be. Ain't that right, Nola?"

"Sure, Ben. Whatever you say." *You bastard.*

"I believe I'll have me another drink, and then I got to be goin', sweetheart. You know me—I got places to go and things to be doin'."

Nola reached for the bottle and the glass. Mallory was looking at her expectantly as he waited for her to pour the drink. Cool and calm despite the pain she felt and the storm of emotions that was raging inside her, Nola did just that.

She didn't spill a drop.


Longarm was dressed and sitting in one of the comfortable armchairs in Nola's room, reading the rest of the newspaper. He glanced up as she came in, then lowered the paper and looked again at her, feeling his insides go taut with fury. The bruises on her face told the story plain as day.

Somebody had slapped the hell out of her.

"Mallory," he said. Somehow, he just knew.

Nola nodded and took a deep, shaky breath. "I know you must've come here after Mallory, Custis," she said. "And I'm ready to do anything you want to help you get him. Anything at all."

98

# Chapter 12

When she had told him what had happened downstairs, Longarm didn't see any point in keeping the truth from Nola any longer. "You're right," he told her. "I came here looking for Mallory and his gang because they've been holding up stagecoaches and stealing silver shipments from the mailbags." He held up the copy of the *Bugle* so that she could see the headline. "He was busy doing just that the past couple of days, and I reckon that's why it took him until now to come in here and rough you up for shooting his man the other day."

Nola took a deep breath. "I knew he was a bastard. I knew he was an outlaw. I didn't know he was such a cold-blooded killer, too. But I don't have any trouble believing it," she added grimly. "Not one bit."

Longarm stood up, went to her, put his hands on her shoulders. "I'm sorry about what he did to you."

"No need for you to be sorry," she said with a shake of her head. "You didn't have anything to do with this, Custis. I can see how you might feel bad about Mrs. Keegan and even Dupree, but you didn't have anything to do with Mallory slapping me around. That was just him being a no-good bastard, as usual."

Longarm nodded. "I reckon you're right."

99

"Well. What do we do now?"

"*We* don't do anything. But it's time that I got back to my job, which is bringing in Mallory and recovering as much of the stolen loot as I can."

"I can help you do that when the time comes," said Nola, "but you're not ready yet, Custis. It's been less than a week since you were shot."

"I just lost a little blood," he protested. "That bullet didn't scramble up my insides none."

"You still need to get more of your strength back before you go after Mallory." Nola smiled suddenly, as if an idea had just occurred to her. "And I can help by finding out where he's stashed the silver the gang has already stolen."

Longarm frowned. "How are you going to do that?"

Lightly, Nola touched her bruised cheek. "You wouldn't believe it to look at me now," she said, "but Mallory's got a soft spot where I'm concerned. All I have to do is let him think I'm sorry about what happened with his men, and he'll forget all about being mad at me. Once he's feeling friendly again, I can get the information out of him, I promise you that."

The furrows on Longarm's forehead deepened. "I ain't sure I like the sound of that," he said.

"Custis, I'm a whore, remember?" she said bluntly. "Worse men than Mallory have bedded me. It doesn't have anything to do with . . . with you and me."

Longarm grimaced, but he knew she was at least partially right. "I ain't sure there *is* anybody worse than Mallory," he muttered.

"Oh, yes," she said, and for a moment he heard the hollowness of memory in her voice. "Ben Mallory is an evil bastard and doesn't care who knows it. He doesn't hide his evil behind a face that pretends to care—"

She caught her breath and turned away sharply. Longarm wanted to hug her and tell her it would be all right, but he let the distance between them remain. Sometimes folks just

100

had to be alone with their pain, and he sensed that this was one of those times.

When she turned back to him a moment later, her eyes shone brightly, as if tears lurked there. Her cheeks were dry, however. "Right now I think you should lie down and rest some more," she said briskly. "For now, you just let me worry about Mallory. By the time you've recovered, we'll be ready to make our move."

Grudgingly, he nodded. "All right. But you be mighty careful. It would probably be a good idea, too, not to mention who I really am or what we're up to when you're talking to those gals of yours."

"You mean Angie and Rafaela and Mickey?" Nola smiled. "They think you're some sort of outlaw, that Mallory's men were after you because you were trying to move in on their territory. It would probably be best to let them keep on believing that."

Longarm nodded again. "I wish I could get word to my boss about what's going on, too. I reckon ol' Billy's getting pretty worried by now, even though he wouldn't admit it. But it'd be too chancy to risk a telegram."

"There's no telegraph service here anyway," said Nola. "But you could write a letter if you'd like. Is there anyone you could send it to who would deliver it for you, so that you wouldn't have to address it to the chief marshal?"

Longarm grinned. He knew the address of Henry's rooming house, knew that the young man could be depended upon to pass along a message to Billy Vail. "That's a good idea," he told Nola.

"I'll bring you paper and a pen." She pointed at the bed. "Now rest!"

He put a finger under her chin and tilted her head up so that he could kiss her. "Yes'm," he murmured against her lips. "You're right—I got to get my strength back."

*For more reasons than one*, he thought.

• • •

Mallory didn't come back into the Silver Slipper that evening, but he showed up again the next afternoon, once more in an expansive mood. It was snowing lightly outside, and as Mallory entered the saloon, he took his hat off and slapped the white flakes from it. With a grin, he called loudly, "Drinks are on me!"

That was Mallory's way, Nola thought as she stood at the end of the bar. He ruled Galena City through a combination of largess and sheer terror. He was like an old-time king or emperor whose word was law, who might be generous one minute and the next minute might order someone's head cut off.

She put a smile on her face. The bruises were still there, but they had been covered up with cosmetics today. She moved toward him, and when he noticed her, he threw his arms wide and grinned at her. "Nola! My favorite saloon-keeper!"

She allowed him to embrace her and willed her muscles to relax, rather than tensing in the revulsion that she really felt. "Hello, Ben," she murmured.

"No hard feelin's about what happened yesterday, are there?" he asked.

"Of course not. You were right, and I was wrong."

He kissed her, then said, "That's what I like to hear."

She could feel the eyes of her bartenders and the women who worked for her watching her to see how she was going to handle Mallory. They would take their cues from her. But she knew that they would be at least a little disappointed to see her knuckling under to him.

That couldn't be helped. When the time was right, they would know how she really felt about him. Everyone would know, including Ben Mallory himself. It would be quite a surprise, and she hoped he would take that surprise with him to hell.

"Have a drink with me?" asked Mallory.

"Of course. I'd be glad to." Nola signaled to one of the bartenders, and he put a bottle on the bar in front of her. The whiskey wasn't the usual Who-hit-John, either. It was the good stuff, the stuff that actually matched the label on the bottle. Nola smiled at Mallory and suggested, "Why don't we go over to a table and sit down?"

"That sounds mighty fine to me." He put his arm around her shoulders as she picked up the bottle and a couple of glasses and headed for a table in the corner. As they walked, he reached down and brazenly fondled her breast through her dress.

Nola hoped he couldn't hear her teeth grating together.

They sat down, Mallory hooking one of the chairs with his foot so that he could pull it over close to the one where Nola sat. She eased the cork from the neck of the bottle and poured drinks for them. Mallory picked up his and looked at her expectantly, and she realized he was waiting for her to join him in a toast. She lifted her glass.

Mallory clinked them together. "To good times," he said.

"To good times," echoed Nola. *Let's see . . . that would be looking down at your sorry corpse.*

He could see none of that thought on her face. She'd had years of experience at hiding what she was really feeling, going all the way back to the time when she was a child and—

No, she told herself, she had enough to worry about now without going back that far in her memory. She smiled, sipped the whiskey, and asked, "What have you been doing lately, Ben? We haven't seen as much of you around here as usual."

"I'm a busy man, you know that. Always got plenty to do."

"So I've heard."

He frowned, and for a second she worried that she had gone too far. "What do you mean by that?" he demanded.

"Just that everyone talks about what a clever man you are, and how strong, too, the way you keep those men of yours in line."

That was laying it on awfully thick, but Mallory had always been susceptible to flattery. It worked this time, too, as he grinned and said, "Yep, I reckon I'm pretty smart, and I don't let anybody get away with crossin' me. That's why I had to rough you up a little. People got to show me the proper respect."

Nola nodded and said, "That's right. And the stronger you are, the more money you have, the more people respect you."

Mallory tossed off the rest of the drink and poured himself another one. "Damn right. I reckon you've heard the old saying about the golden rule."

Nola arched her eyebrows curiously.

"Him that has the gold, rules!" Mallory cackled and slapped the table with an open hand. The slap sounded almost like a gunshot. He was clearly delighted with himself. He leaned back in his chair and tilted the glass to his lips again, and when he lowered it, he said, "Only in my case, it's silver I got plenty of, not gold."

"What did you do, buy a mine?"

"Hell, you ought to know better'n that, Nola! Do you really think I'm goin' to grub around in a hole in the ground to dig the stuff up when I can wait for somebody else to do it for me?"

Nola allowed a worried look to appear on her face. She didn't want to seem too curious about his business. "Maybe you'd better not tell me any more, Ben. I might be better off not knowing."

"I'll tell you anything I want," he snapped. He wasn't happy about her trying to stop his boasting. "The same way as I take anything I want. The fellas who run those mines thought they were so damned smart, hidin' their silver in mailbags and shippin' it out on the stagecoaches. Well, I showed 'em how smart they really are! That silver they worked so hard for is mine now, and I got it stashed where they'll never find it!"

He polished off the second drink, tipped the bottle and splashed more whiskey into the glass. Nola had never seen him really drunk, but whiskey did loosen his tongue to a certain extent. She had been counting on that tendency, and it was holding true so far. If she could keep him drinking, that and his sheer arrogance might be enough to make him reveal the things she wanted to know.

She nodded and said, "I figured you might have a hideout somewhere up in the mountains."

"Yeah, it's a place where nobody can bother us. Not the whites, not the Paiutes, not anybody alive. And I never been afraid of dead folks!"

Nola wasn't sure what he meant by that, but at least it was a start. He had admitted that he and his gang were responsible for the silver robberies, and he had given her a hint as to where the stolen loot was hidden. When she reported this conversation to Custis, maybe he could figure out what Mallory meant.

Mallory threw back his third drink, then surprised her by reaching over and grasping her wrist. "I'm tired of talkin'," he said. "Why don't we go upstairs?"

Despite her brave words to Custis about being bedded by worse men than Mallory, Nola's skin crawled at the thought of letting him have her again after what he had done. She forced a bright smile onto her face and used her free hand to nudge the bottle closer to Mallory.

"I thought we'd finish this off," she said. "No use leaving a soldier only wounded."

Mallory kept one hand on Nola's wrist and used the other to pick up the cork and jam it back into the neck of the bottle. "Nope," he declared. "I've had enough panther piss for now. What I ain't had enough of lately is you, darlin'."

Nola didn't see any way out of this predicament short of going to bed with him. She didn't want to make him angry again. The success of the plans she and Custis had begun to hatch depended on keeping Mallory feeling friendly toward her for a while longer.

Determinedly, she kept smiling and said, "All right."

"That's more like it." Mallory came to his feet and pulled

her up with him, his grip tightening on her wrist. "Come on."

He led her toward the stairs. Nola felt empty inside, knowing that the bartenders and her girls and all the customers in the Silver Slipper were watching. They all knew where Mallory was taking her, too, and why.

The life she had led, whether it was truly her choice or not, had never really bothered her before. Things were the way they were, and it was up to her to make the best of them.

But now, after meeting Custis Long and getting to know him, her attitude had subtly changed. Custis had his rough edges, but he was a good man, an honest man. She knew, as well, that he would never judge her for the things she had done in her life in order to survive.

No, Custis wouldn't judge her . . . but that didn't stop Nola from judging herself, and for the first time in years, she was starting to find herself lacking.

When she and Mallory reached the top of the stairs, Nola turned to the left, rather than the right. There was an empty room down the corridor in this direction that they could use.

She was hoping that Mallory wouldn't notice the change, but he tugged at her wrist and said, "Hey, where are we goin'? Your room's the other way."

"I've had to move out of that room for now," she said. "There are, ah, rats in it."

Mallory grinned, pulled his Colt from its holster, and twirled it on one finger like some kid from a Wild West Show. "Just show me them rats, and I'll blow their damned heads off!"

"No, that's all right." Nola tried to steer him the other direction. "I already have traps set. You wouldn't want to accidentally step on one of them."

"I reckon not." Mallory holstered his gun. "Well, let's go. I don't really care where it is, long as I get to poke you when we get there."

Somehow, Nola kept smiling . . .

# Chapter 13

Longarm was cleaning his gun when Nola came into the room. He hadn't used the Colt in a week, and cleaning it made him feel as if he was at least accomplishing something. Ever since he had awakened that morning, impatience had been growing inside him. Yes, he was still a little weak, he supposed, and if he moved too quickly or turned in the wrong way, his side hurt where the bullet had ripped through it.

But despite all that, damn it, it was time for him to get back to work! He had been laid up before, and he had always hated every minute of it whenever a job was left undone. The only times he could truly relax were between assignments from Billy Vail.

So he supposed he looked a little eager when Nola came in and said, "Mallory was here."

Longarm snapped the revolver's cylinder closed. "Is he still around?"

She shook her head and looked away from him. "No, he left a few minutes ago."

"Blast it," said Longarm as he got to his feet, "you should've got word to me somehow—"

"Why?" she broke in as she turned sharply back toward him. "So you could have come busting in while he actually had me in bed with him?"

Longarm frowned. Despite what Nola had said the day before, obviously she didn't like the part she was now being forced to play with Mallory. He couldn't blame her for that. He had never liked the idea from the start, in fact.

"Listen," he said, "you don't have to do that again. Mallory's my job—"

She stopped him again, this time with a sigh and a wave of her hand. "I'm sorry, Custis. I didn't mean for you to see how upset I am. Anyway, I found out some of the things we wanted to know. Mallory and his gang are definitely behind the silver robberies. He practically admitted as much to me."

Longarm slid the Colt back into its holster and set the coiled gunbelt on the small table next to the chair where he had been sitting. He stepped over to Nola and drew her into his arms. "That's what we figured," he said. "You didn't have to play up to him just to find that out."

"There's more," said Nola as she looked up at him. "He told me that his hideout is in the mountains somewhere. He said that the whites don't bother him there, or the Paiutes, and that he isn't afraid of dead people. What do you think he meant by that?"

It took a few moments of thinking, of casting his mind back over the trails he had ridden in the past, before Longarm had the answer. Nola had never been in these parts until she came to Galena City to open the Silver Slipper. If she had spent more time in this corner of Nevada, she might have come up with the same thought as Longarm.

"There's a place up toward Virginia Peak where the Paiutes used to bury their dead," Longarm said. "They won't come near the place, and there's no silver thereabouts, so the whites don't have any reason to be there, either. That sure sounds to me like it might be where Mallory is talking about."

Nola cocked her head. "An Indian burial ground? You must be right, Custis. No one would think of looking for Mallory there."

"Is that where he's got the loot from the other robberies stashed?"

She nodded and said, "I think so."

Longarm rasped a thumbnail along his jaw as he frowned in thought. "Mallory probably leaves some of his men up there all the time, even when he comes into town," he mused. "He wouldn't want to ride off and leave all that silver unguarded." He shrugged. "Well, we'll chew that bite of the apple when we come to it. For now, I reckon we have to concentrate on dabbing a loop on Mallory himself."

"You mean setting a trap for him."

"That's right," said Longarm. "I did some cowboying for a few years after the Late Unpleasantness, and sometimes the way we talked then still comes out in me. A trap is exactly what I've got in mind, and I've already been doing some thinking about how to set it. One thing's for sure—we know the best bait for Mallory. Silver."

Nola was thinking, too. She said, "If Mallory thought that a big shipment was about to go out—"

"He'd be there waiting for it," Longarm finished for her.

"So all we have to do—"

"Me," Longarm broke in. "Not you, Nola, just me. I have to be waiting for Mallory when he tries to hit the stagecoach the silver is supposed to be on. But it'll be your job to plant the idea in his head and make sure he comes after the right coach."

"I can do that," she said confidently, "but it worries me, Custis, the idea of you trying to capture Mallory by yourself. You're just starting to recover from that gunshot wound."

"I'll be fine," Longarm assured her. He drew her into his arms again and kissed her lightly on the lips. "After the way you've taken care of me for the past week, I feel like a whole new man."

That wasn't completely true. Longarm knew he wasn't back to full strength yet. But it would take a while to set up the trap for Ben Mallory, and by the time the trap was ready

109

to close, Longarm was confident he would be there, waiting to see Mallory caught in it.

Before the gunfight with Mallory's men had left him wounded and lying low in the Silver Slipper, Longarm hadn't had a chance to talk to the manager of the stage station in Galena City. He would have gotten around to it if a bullet hadn't gotten in his way. Now it was time to have a long parley with the man.

"His name is Claude Jessup," Nola told Longarm as they discussed their plans. "He comes in occasionally for a drink, but he never goes upstairs with one of the girls."

"You reckon you could get him up here to talk to me?" asked Longarm. "If you could get word to him that I had a message from his boss, Bat Thompson, down in Carson City, that might do the trick."

Nola smiled. "Don't worry, I can talk just about any man into doing what I want, Custis, without him even knowing I'm doing it. Not all men are as stubborn and hardheaded as you are."

"I'll take that as a compliment . . . I think. I need to talk to Jessup as soon as you can manage it."

Nola nodded and said again, "Don't worry about a thing."

She was as good as her word. Less than an hour after she'd gone back downstairs, she returned, opening the door of her bedroom and stepping in with a balding, burly, middle-aged man arm in arm with her. He was laughing, but he stopped short and the pleased expression vanished abruptly from his face as he saw Longarm standing up from an armchair. "What's this?" he asked sharply. "Nola, you didn't say anything about another man! If this is a robbery—"

"Hold on, old son," Longarm said as he held up a hand, palm out. "Nola didn't bring you up here so that we could rob you. In fact, I'm a lawman."

"A lawman!" exclaimed Jessup. "What's this all about?"

"If Nola will shut the door, I'll tell you." When Nola had closed the door to the corridor, Longarm went on quietly. "I

110

thought you were going to tell Mr. Jessup here that I had a message from his boss.''

She shrugged. ''That wasn't necessary. It seems that Mr. Jessup was more than willing to come upstairs. It was just that no one had ever asked him.'' She frowned in mock severity. ''I'm going to have to have a talk with those girls of mine.''

Jessup looked totally confused. ''What's going on here?'' he demanded. ''If you're a lawman, mister, where's your badge?''

Longarm held up the leather folder. ''Right here,'' he said as he tossed it to Jessup. ''Have a look for yourself.''

The manager of the stagecoach station seemed satisfied by the badge and the identification documents in the folder. He crossed the room and handed it back to Longarm. ''All right, Marshal Long,'' he said. ''I suppose I believe you. But why all this secrecy?''

''Ben Mallory thinks I'm dead,'' Longarm said bluntly, ''and I'd just as soon keep it that way.''

Jessup's eyes widened as a realization dawned on him. ''You're the man who shot that miner. You're the one they say killed Mrs. Keegan!''

Longarm shook his head vehemently. ''They can say anything they want, but I never hurt that poor woman. Mallory's men did that. And yeah, I shot that miner, but only after he took a shot at me and wounded that newspaper fella instead. He wanted to give up mining and join Mallory's gang. Thought it he bushwhacked me, it would give him an in with Mallory.''

''I reckon it could've happened that way,'' Jessup said dubiously. ''It doesn't seem much like a U.S. marshal would really do the things you've been accused of.''

''That's right. I would have talked to you sooner, Mr. Jessup, but I caught a bullet from one of Mallory's boys not long after I got into town, and I've been holed up here in the Silver Slipper ever since.''

111

Jessup glanced at Nola, grunted, and said, "I suppose there's plenty of worse places to hide out."

"That's mighty true," replied Longarm with a grin. "But I'm getting back on my feet, and I'm ready to go after Mallory again. That's where you come in."

Jessup looked surprised. "You want to, what, deputize me or something?"

"Nope. I just need your help in setting up a trap for Mallory."

"Then I'm your man," said Jessup with a curt nod. "I'll do anything you want, Marshal, if it'll help bring that bastard to justice." He glanced at Nola. "Beggin' your pardon for my language, ma'am."

"That's all right, Claude," Nola told him. "Mallory *is* a bastard. A gold-plated one, in fact."

Longarm couldn't have agreed more, but he didn't want to waste time standing around talking about what a sorry son Mallory was. He said, "I talked to your boss, old Bat Thompson, down in Carson City, but he didn't tell me what the schedule is up here in these parts. How often do the coaches run to and from Galena City?"

"Twice a week," replied Jessup. "This is the end of the line, so when the coach gets here it just turns around and heads back to Virginia City and then on down to Carson City. The schedule calls for the coaches to roll in every Sunday and Wednesday at noon, and by God, we stick to it." There was pride in his voice.

Longarm nodded, then realized that despite his best intentions, he had lost track of what day it was. That was easy to do when all a fella had to do was laze around and be waited on hand and foot by beautiful women. He looked at Nola and asked, "What day is it?"

"Monday," she said. "The stagecoach left yesterday."

"Won't be another until Wednesday noon," added Jessup.

Longarm accepted the information with another nod. That worked out pretty well, he thought. He would have a couple of days to set the snare for Mallory.

"Have any of the mines around here shipped out any silver lately?" he asked.

Jessup shook his head. "Not for several weeks. They're all scared that it won't get through."

"Well," said Longarm, "that's about to change . . ."

The plan depended on Mallory coming into the Silver Slipper before the stagecoach made its run on Wednesday. Longarm sweated that out, and when Mallory didn't appear on Monday night, his worry grew. Of course, if Mallory didn't show up on Tuesday, the plan could still be put into effect a few days later, using the coach that would arrive in Galena City at noon on Sunday.

But Longarm was impatient and more than ready to nab Mallory in the act of holding up the stagecoach. Any extra delay was going to eat at him.

Nola knew how he felt, and so she was grateful when she looked up from her place at the end of the bar on Tuesday evening and saw Mallory sauntering into the saloon, trailed by several of his men.

They headed for the bar, and immediately the drinkers there moved aside nervously to make room for the outlaws. Mallory tossed a double eagle onto the hardwood and said loudly to the bartender, "Give my boys whatever they want, barkeep." Then he looked at Nola and grinned. He strolled along the bar to join her.

"Hello, Ben," she greeted him with a smile. "It's good to see you again."

His dark eyes played over her body, lingering on the valley between her breasts, visible in the low-cut gown she wore. "You're lookin' mighty nice, Nola," he said. "Feelin' friendly tonight, are you?"

She leaned against him and toyed with his cowhide vest with one hand. "Of course," she murmured, her voice almost a purr. "You always make me feel friendly, Ben."

"Well, I'd say you've learned your lesson right well,

113

then." He sounded smugly satisfied with himself. "I'll be takin' you upstairs in a little bit."

"Whatever you say, Ben," she told him, still smiling, still keeping a tight rein on the way she really felt.

"Lemme get a drink or two first." Mallory signaled curtly to the bartender.

"Bring the bottle," Nola said to the man. To Mallory, she added, "Let's go over to a table. I've got something to tell you."

He arched his bushy eyebrows curiously but reached out to snag the bottle and the glasses the bartender brought. When he and Nola were seated at a table in the rear corner of the saloon, he asked, "Now, what's all this about?"

Nola didn't answer until she had poured the drinks for them. She sipped hers, then said, "I know about you, Ben."

Instantly, suspicion flickered in his eyes. "What do you know?" he demanded.

"That you're a smart man."

That mollified Mallory slightly. "Damn right I am," he said.

"Smart enough to appreciate a smart woman."

Mallory shrugged, waited for her to go on.

"I heard something earlier today I think you might be interested in," continued Nola. "You know how men like to talk when they come into a saloon. Well, Charlie Dodson was in here, and he said the Calamity is about to ship some silver out on tomorrow's coach. Several weeks' worth, in fact."

The Calamity Mine was the biggest of the silver mines in the area surrounding Galena City, and Charlie Dodson was the superintendent. Mallory leaned forward eagerly as he heard what Nola said.

"You sure about that?" he asked.

Nola nodded. "I'm certain. He was telling Mr. Dupree about it."

Mallory tossed down his drink, then leaned back in his chair and rubbed his angular jaw as he frowned in thought.

After a moment, he said, "Why are you tellin' me about this?"

It was Nola's turn to shrug. "I just thought you might like to know, that's all."

Slowly, a grin spread across Mallory's face. "You know, I reckon you are a pretty smart woman, just like you said, Nola. Maybe I should have started listenin' to you before now. Here in this saloon, you hear all the good gossip in town, don't you?"

"It's hard for anything to happen around here that I don't know about ahead of time," she said meaningfully.

Mallory gave an abrupt nod. "Much obliged for the information." He poured himself another drink, tossed it down. Then he scraped his chair back and stood up.

"We're going upstairs now?" asked Nola.

Mallory shook his head. "Not tonight. I got to talk to the rest of the boys and do some thinkin'. Sorry, Nola."

She made a little pout of disappointment. Sarah Bernhardt and Lillie Langtry didn't have anything on her when it came to acting, she thought. "I suppose I'll get over it," she said with a sigh.

Mallory grinned and leaned over to chuck her under the chin. "Don't you worry, I'll be comin' to see you again," he promised. "Hell, if everything works out, I might even bring you a present next time."

"I'd like that, Ben." But the best present of all would be seeing him either behind bars or kicking out his life at the end of a hangrope.

Mallory went back to the bar and talked in low, urgent tones to his men for a few minutes. Then all of them left, going out into the cold night and slamming the door after them, and a sigh of relief seemed to go through the whole saloon.

Nola headed upstairs.

Longarm was waiting in Nola's room along with Claude Jessup, J. Emerson Dupree, and a thick-bodied man with gray-

115

ing, sandy hair who had been introduced to him by Jessup as Charlie Dodson, the superintendent of the Calamity Mine. Dupree had been shocked to see that Longarm was still alive when Jessup brought him and Dodson to the Silver Slipper, but his newspaperman's instincts were whetted by the news that Longarm was really a U.S. marshal. The four men were sitting around and talking in quiet tones when the door opened and Nola stepped in. She shut the door behind her and smiled at the men who watched her expectantly.

"He took the bait," she said. "Swallowed it hook, line, and sinker."

# Chapter 14

The cot in the back room of the stagecoach station wasn't nearly as comfortable as Nola's bed, but Longarm made do. He was too excited to sleep much, anyway. His head was full of the plan that he hoped would finally rope in Ben Mallory.

Longarm didn't particularly like bringing so many people in on it, but there was no way to set things up properly otherwise. Dupree and Dodson had had a long conversation at the bar downstairs, so that if Mallory asked anyone, the honest answer would be that the newspaperman and the mine superintendent had indeed been talking earlier in the evening. That lent credence to the story Nola had told Mallory.

Then, after Mallory had taken the bait just as Longarm hoped he would, Longarm had waited until well after midnight to leave the saloon and walk quickly through the back alleys of Galena City with Jessup. Dupree and Dodson had already gone back to the *Bugle* and the Calamity, respectively, just as they would have normally.

The waiting came next, and that was always the hardest part for Longarm. He went over and over the plan in his mind, looking for weak spots. He didn't see any. Surprise was the main thing on his side. He intended to put it to good use.

Longarm finally slept some, but he was awake early the next morning. His breath fogged in the air as he moved around. It was cold in the station, since he'd had to let the fire in the stove go out. Jessup lived in a small cabin not far away, so the station itself was supposed to be empty at night. Longarm had maintained that illusion, but in the process he had gotten thoroughly chilled. He was mighty glad when Jessup arrived for the day carrying a small package. The stationmaster started a fire in the stove and put a pot of coffee on to brew. Longarm stayed in the back room most of the time, just in case anyone came into the station before the stage arrived.

It appeared that no one was leaving Galena City today, though, since nobody showed up to buy a ticket and wait for the stage. The only visitor was Charlie Dodson, who pulled up behind the building in a wagon about mid-morning. Jessup went out to meet him, and a few minutes later the two men came back inside. Each of them was carrying a canvas bag that looked heavy.

Dodson nodded a greeting to Longarm, then pointed at the bags and said with a grin, "Rocks. That's all."

"That'll do," said Longarm. "If Mallory has a man keeping an eye on the station this morning, it'll look like the two of you just carried in a shipment of ingots."

"We'll split 'em up in the mailbags, just like you planned," said Jessup. "That way the bags'll look heavy enough when we load 'em on the stage."

"Looks to me like you've got everything figured out, Marshal," commented Dodson. "The only thing I don't understand is how you intend to get the drop on Mallory and his whole gang. They'll have you outgunned."

Longarm picked up the package Jessup had brought into the station earlier. "That's where this comes in. It's dynamite."

"I got it at the hardware store," said Jessup. "Told the clerk I needed to blow up a stump out back." He shrugged.

"If there's any left over when the marshal gets back, I might just use it for that."

"Mallory won't expect to have a few sticks of this hellish stuff flung into the middle of his bunch from the coach," Longarm said as he hefted the package of dynamite. "That ought to put some of the gang down and shake up the rest so that I can make them drop their guns. That's what I'm counting on, anyway."

"Dynamite's not too careful what it blows up," Dodson pointed out. "Could be you'll get Mallory himself."

Longarm shrugged. "If that's the way it works out, then so be it. I'd rather see him stand trial and hang, but the main thing is to put a stop to these robberies."

"Amen to that," Dodson said fervently. "Well, it seems like you've got everything under control." He shook hands with Longarm. "Good luck, Marshal."

"Likely I'll need it," said Longarm dryly.

He just didn't know how much.

The time remaining until the stagecoach arrived dragged by. Jessup prepared the mailbags, taking the rocks from the bags Dodson had brought and loading them into the large canvas pouches marked U.S. Mail. Longarm drank coffee and gnawed on one of the biscuits Jessup had brought from home. The wound in his side ached, but only a little. The bandages had been changed the night before by Rafaela, before Longarm had left the Silver Slipper, and the brunette had pronounced her approval of the healing process. The bullet holes hurt less now and itched more, and Longarm knew that was a good sign.

There was a banjo clock on the wall of the station's front room, much like the one in Billy Vail's office back in Denver. Longarm wondered if Vail had gotten the letter he'd sent in care of Henry. He lounged in the doorway between the rooms and looked at the clock, willing the hands to move faster. They were almost straight up at noon when Jessup

119

glanced through the window at the street and said, "Uh-oh, what's all this?"

Longarm almost stepped to his side, then hung back, not wanting anyone to see him peering out the window and possibly recognize him. "What is it?" he asked tensely.

Jessup turned to look at him, a worried look on his face. "Miss Nola's coming along the boardwalk, and she's got some of her girls with her. They look like they're headed here, and they're dressed for traveling."

"Damn it!" Longarm pulled his hat down so that it would conceal most of his face and stepped to the window to chance a quick look. Jessup was right: Nola was on her way, flanked by Angie, Rafaela, and Mickey. All four of the women were wearing traveling outfits and had hats pinned to their upswept hair. They were carrying carpetbags, too. Longarm muttered, "What the hell do they think they're doing?"

A moment later the door of the station opened, and Nola swept in imperiously, followed by the other three young women. Longarm stayed where he was; there was no point in hiding from them, since they all knew he was still alive anyway.

"Good morning, Claude," Nola said with a smile. "The Wednesday stage ought to be here any minute, shouldn't it?"

Jessup glanced at Longarm and swallowed nervously when he saw the big lawman's grim expression. But there was nothing he could do except nod in response to Nola's question and say, "Yes, ma'am, that's right. Any minute now."

"What do you think you're doing, Nola?" Longarm asked tautly.

She turned a level gaze on him, and he could read nothing there but determination. "Why, we're going to Virginia City," she said. "We make the trip occasionally to do some shopping, don't we, Claude?"

Jessup swallowed again, obviously aware that he was caught between a rock and a hard place. "It's true, Marshal," he said. "The ladies go to Virginia City about once a month, and it's been a while since they were there."

"So no one will think there's anything unusual about us getting on that stage," said Nola.

Longarm took a deep breath and tried to rein in his anger. "You can't go," he said flatly. "You know that."

"I know nothing of the sort," Nola shot back at him. "When Mallory and his men stop the stage, you're liable to need help, Custis."

Longarm glanced at Angie, Rafaela, and Mickey, unsure of how much Nola had told them about the plan—and about him.

Nola must have understood what the look meant, because she said, "They know all about it, and all about you, too, Custis."

"Yeah," put in Angie with a grin. "I've heard of you, Marshal. You're the one they call Longarm." She gave a bawdy laugh. "And I reckon I know one reason why they call you that, too."

Longarm bit back an annoyed curse. He didn't have time for this. He glanced at the banjo clock, saw that the hands were now straight up. The stage would soon be here . . .

Jessup glanced through the window and said, "Here it comes."

"Four tickets to Virginia City, Claude," Nola said briskly. "Round trip."

Jessup glanced at Longarm and said, "What do I do, Marshal?"

Longarm hesitated a moment, then growled, "Sell 'em the damn tickets." He added to Nola and the other women, "Keep your heads down when the shooting starts, all of you. I won't have time to be worrying about you."

"You won't have to worry about us, Custis," said Nola. "I think I can promise you that much."

Longarm sighed heavily. Despite what he had said, he knew that when the time came, he *would* worry about them. He wouldn't be able to help himself. Nola had saved his life, and the other three women had helped nurse him back to health. Now he would not only have to capture or kill Mallory and the rest of the gang, but he would have to keep the women safe, too.

*Well, old son*, he told himself, *you knew the job was damned hard work when you first pinned on that badge* . . .

Jessup punched four tickets and handed them to Nola, who paid him for them. Then he stepped out onto the porch of the station to greet the stage as it pulled up. Longarm glanced through the window and saw that the two men on the driver's box were the same ones who had worked the run from Carson City down to Tonopah when he made that trip. The jehu named George was handling the reins, and the duster-clad youngster called Pryor was sitting beside him, cradling a greener in his lap. Bat Thompson had said they were good men to have around in case of trouble, and Longarm was glad to see them.

Longarm heard Jessup say, according to the plan, "Take 'er on around back to the barn, George. We'll swap teams there. I want to check them thoroughbraces."

George looked a little puzzled by the request, but he nodded. "Sure, Claude, whatever you say," he replied as he slapped the reins against the backs of the team and got the horses moving again.

The coach rolled on around the station to the large barn, and Jessup went out the back door. Longarm crossed his arms and regarded Nola and the other women balefully. Angie came over and punched him lightly on the shoulder. "Aw, hell, Custis, don't look so mad," she said. "It'll be all right. You don't have to worry about us. We can take care of ourselves. Ain't that right, girls?"

Rafaela said quietly, "After some of the things we've seen and done, Marshal, going up against some outlaws doesn't seem like a whole hell of a lot."

"You're not going up against any outlaws," snapped Longarm. "You're going to keep your heads down and let me handle Mallory and his bunch, just like I said. Hell, there's not really any reason for any of you to go along."

"We want to be sure you're all right, Custis," Nola said.

"We have quite an investment in you, you know."

Rafaela said, "You've been eating our food and drinking our coffee and whiskey for over a week, you know."

"Not to mention anything else you've been getting from Nola," said Angie with a grin that didn't falter even when Nola scowled at her.

"All right," Longarm said, not wanting them to start arguing. "I reckon I can understand why you don't want me to get shot up again. Just . . . be careful."

Nola nodded. "We will be, Custis. I promise."

Jessup came in the back of the station. He was carrying Pryor's duster. He handed the long coat to Longarm as he said to Nola and her companions, "Ladies, you can board the stage as soon as we bring it around to the front of the building again."

Longarm slipped the duster on over his sheepskin jacket. Bringing it in had been a good idea on Jessup's part. It was unlikely that Mallory had anyone watching the station, but just in case there was a spy, the duster might throw him off. He could easily mistake Longarm for Pryor, since their hats were similar and they were about the same size.

Longarm picked up one of the mailbags while Jessup hefted the other one. With his head down, Longarm walked out the rear door of the station and crossed the short distance to the barn. Jessup walked alongside him, carrying the other bag. As soon as they were inside, safe from any prying eyes, Longarm handed the mailbag up to George, who stowed it in the boot under the driver's box. Then Longarm stripped off the duster and gave it back to the waiting shotgun guard. "Much obliged for the loan," he said to Pryor.

The young man grinned. "Claude told us all about what's going on here, Marshal. We'll do whatever it takes to put a stop to Mallory's depredations."

George spat from atop the driver's box, then drawled, "The kid reads. That's why he talks like that."

"I been known to frequent the Denver library myself," said Longarm as he returned Pryor's grin. "Especially along

123

toward the end of the month when my money's running low and it ain't payday yet.''

Jessup handed the other mailbag to George, then turned to Longarm. ''Best climb inside,'' he said. ''George'll take the coach back around front and pick up the rest of the passengers.''

Longarm shook his head as he reached up to open the door of the coach. ''Nope. Just drive on and leave 'em here. They won't like it when they find out they've been left behind—''

''We certainly wouldn't,'' Nola's voice said from the door of the barn. ''That's why we decided to come on out here and board the stage.''

The four men looked around in surprise and watched the women daintily walk along the broad aisle that ran down the center of the barn. Longarm grimaced. He had hoped to slip that trick past Nola, but he realized now that he had underestimated her. A gal in her line of work had to be used to men lying to her, so she would be naturally suspicious of everything.

''I still say it's a damned bad idea—'' he began.

''Not as bad as letting you go off on your own and get shot up by a bunch of outlaws,'' Nola said stubbornly as she reached his side. She held out a gloved hand. ''Now, if you would be so kind as to assist me, Marshal . . .''

Longarm sighed and took her hand. He helped her into the coach and would have assisted the other women as well, but he saw that young Pryor had already snatched off his hat and had taken Angie's hand. She was cooing and making eyes at him as he led her around to the door on the other side of the coach. Rafaela and Mickey followed.

Jessup shook hands with Longarm and said, ''Good luck, Marshal,'' just as Charlie Dodson had done a couple of hours earlier.

And just as he had done then, Longarm thought that he was going to need it.

Now, more than ever.

# Chapter 15

Under other circumstances, it would have been mighty pleasant to sit inside a stagecoach with four beautiful ladies and rock along a mountain road on a crisp, clear day like this. The clouds had finally blown away, and this Nevada high country was as beautiful as Longarm had ever seen it.

Of course, he couldn't really see much of it, because he was sitting on the floor of the coach between the two seats, his hat off and his back propped against one of the doors. That way, if Mallory or anybody else was studying the coach through a telescope or field glasses, they wouldn't be able to see him.

"How are you feeling, Custis?" asked Nola as the coach swayed gently on its thoroughbraces.

"Fine," he replied. "I'm bandaged up so tight nothing can happen to that wound." He nodded to Rafaela. "You did a good job. All of you have. No man could ever ask for better nurses than I've had this past week—or prettier ones, neither." He grinned at Angie.

"Oh, go on with you," she said. "Nola and Mickey and Rafaela are lots prettier than me. I'm like a big ol' plow horse, and they're quarter horses."

Nola patted her hand. "You're a very pretty girl, Angie. You ought to know that by now, the way those miners clamor over you and practically come to blows.''

"Shoot, most of those miners would hump a mountain lion if it'd stay still—''

A thump on the coach roof brought a sudden end to the banter. George called back, "We're comin' up on a bad spot. The road goes through a draw up ahead. It's narrow, and there's plenty of cover on both slopes.''

Longarm remembered the place from his ride up to Galena City. The road was narrow to start with, but even more constricted in the approaching draw. The place was tailor-made for an ambush, all right.

He drew his Winchester closer beside him on the floor of the coach and then reached for the pouch full of dynamite. With a grim-faced glance around at the four women, he said, "You ladies be ready for trouble now. If there's any shooting, I want you down on this floor. I'll be up and out of the way by then.''

"You're calling the shots, Custis,'' said Nola.

Something about her voice bothered him, but when he glanced at her again, she wore a serious, concerned look on her face. She didn't look like she was up to anything.

But she was a woman, Longarm reminded himself, and trying to figure out a woman was like trying to read Sanskrit or one of those other dead languages—most fellas didn't have a clue how to go about it.

It was too late to worry now. Instead, he slipped several of the sticks of dynamite out of the bag and gripped them in his left hand. Then he reached into his shirt pocket and brought out a cheroot and a lucifer. He put the cheroot in his mouth and then turned his head so that he could hold it well away from the dynamite as he lit it. He flicked the lucifer into life and held the flame to the end of the tube of tobacco, sucking in until he had a brightly glowing coal on the end of the cheroot. He pinched out the lucifer and dropped it on the floor of the coach. A long drag on the cheroot helped settle his nerves a little.

That didn't last long, because a moment later the coach

126

rattled into the draw, and a second after that the whipcrack of a rifle shot shattered the peaceful stillness of the afternoon.

"Son of a bitch!" yelled George, and Longarm wondered if the driver was hit. George sounded more angry than he did hurt, however, as he continued to curse. The coach lurched heavily and came to an abrupt stop.

"They killed one of the leaders!" That was Pryor, letting Longarm know what had happened. "They're coming down the slopes on both sides of the draw!"

"Damn it!" Longarm had been worried about something like that. It would make things more difficult, since the outlaws would have the coach caught in a crossfire.

Suddenly, Nola thrust her hand out. "Give me some of that dynamite, Custis! I could always throw a rock as good as any boy when I was a little girl."

Longarm hesitated, then gave Nola the dynamite he had already taken from the bag. Hurriedly, he delved into it again and brought out three more sticks. Outside the coach, men were whooping and shouting and shooting, but Longarm hadn't heard any bullets hit the coach yet. A man's voice yelled, "Drop those guns, boys, and nobody'll get hurt!"

He looked at Nola. She mouthed *Mallory*.

Longarm gave her a curt nod, then drew in hard on the cheroot. The tip glowed a bright cherry-red. He held the fuse of one of the sticks of dynamite to the coal, and it sputtered into life. At the same time, Nola leaned over and held the fuse of one of her sticks to the cheroot. That fuse lit an instant after the first one.

"Now!" Longarm growled around the cheroot.

He rose up, twisted, and flung the dynamite out the window on the near side of the coach. Nola threw her stick out the other window. Longarm had cut the fuses almost dangerously short. He caught a glimpse of the greasy red cylinder turning over and over as it flew through the air. Half a dozen men on horseback were clustered on that side of the coach, and a couple of them yelled in alarm.

127

Then, like twin peals of thunder, both sticks of dynamite blew.

Longarm snatched up the Winchester as two of the outlaws went flying out of their saddles. He didn't know if either of them was Mallory. Time enough to sort that out later. Right now, he was more concerned with corralling the rest of the gang. He stuck the barrel of the rifle through the window in the door and yelled, "Drop your guns! You're under arrest!"

Behind him, surprisingly close, a pistol cracked. "Get 'em, girls!" ordered Nola.

Longarm grated a curse and glanced over his shoulder. Nola, Angie, Rafaela, and Mickey had all hauled guns out of their handbags; they ranged from the small pocket pistol Nola used to an old Dragoon Colt that Angie gripped in both hands as she fired out the window toward the outlaws on the far side of the stagecoach. The noise of guns blasting inside and outside the vehicle was deafening.

A bullet chewed splinters from the door next to Longarm's head, and a couple of the slivers sliced into his cheek and drew his attention back to that side. He opened up with the Winchester. His first shot drove into the chest of one of the outlaws and drove the man backward off his horse like a giant fist.

Longarm jacked the rifle's lever and fired again. He heard the dull boom of Pryor's shotgun and the sharper sound of George's pistol as the two men got into the fight. For a handful of seconds that seemed much longer, guns roared, bullets sang, and the draw was filled with noise and flame and the sharp tang of gun smoke.

Then, with an eerie suddenness like a curtain dropping in a play, the shooting stopped.

Longarm lowered his rifle. All six of the men on his side of the coach were down, but a couple of them were still moving. He heard the door on the other side of the coach open and jerked his head around to see Nola climbing out. "Wait a minute!" he said.

"I think they're all dead," she said, ignoring his order.

The other three women piled out of the coach after her.

Muttering sulfurous curses under his breath, Longarm kicked open the door on his side and dropped to the ground. He kept the muzzle of the Winchester pointing in the general direction of the two outlaws who were definitely still alive. He climbed the pine-dotted slope and checked the other four first, rolling them over with his boot. One of them was alive as well, the breath rasping in the man's throat as he flopped onto his back, arms outflung loosely. There was a bloody streak along the side of his head where a bullet had creased him and knocked him senseless. Longarm moved on to the other two wounded men, kicking their fallen guns well away from their hands before he got too close to them. One of the men was gutshot and probably had only minutes to live. He was writhing in pain but was only semiconscious. The other one had a leg wound and was wide awake—awake enough to cuss a blue streak as Longarm approached him.

"You've broke my leg, you son of a bitch!" he howled.

It looked to Longarm like the bullet had just plowed a furrow in the meaty part of the man's thigh and knocked him out of his saddle. "You'll live, old son," Longarm told him. "Get up and walk down yonder to that coach."

"I can't walk! I'm shot!"

"In that case, I'll just put a bullet through your head so's I won't have to bother with you," Longarm said coldly.

The man cursed some more, but he got hold of a sapling and used it to support himself as he pulled himself to his feet. Wincing and complaining every step of the way, he hobbled down the slope to the bottom of the draw with Longarm following him. The man who had been creased on the head was still out cold, Longarm saw as he went by.

George and Pryor had both climbed down from the box and appeared to be unhurt except for a bullet burn on Pryor's forearm. "They never knew what hit them, Marshal," he said to Longarm with a grin. "That dynamite was a brilliant idea."

Longarm inclined his head toward the other side of the road. "What about the rest of the bunch?"

"We checked 'em out for the ladies," said George. "Got one that's still alive. Looks like a bullet busted his left elbow. He ain't got no fight left in him."

"The rest of them are deceased," added Pryor. "I wasn't aware that the ladies were in possession of an arsenal. It was quite astounding when all that firepower began to demonstrate itself."

"Yeah," said Longarm dryly. "Surprising as all hell." He jerked a thumb at his prisoner, then pointed to the unconscious man on the ground. "Keep an eye on these two. They're the only ones still alive on this side."

George and Pryor nodded.

Longarm walked around the back of the coach. Nola, Angie, Rafaela, and Mickey were gathered on the other side, talking excitedly among themselves. They fell silent when Longarm approached. He frowned at them and said, "I thought I told you ladies to stay down when the shooting started."

"If we'd done that, you might not have captured all the gang," said Nola. "I think we were very helpful."

Longarm couldn't really argue with that. He glanced at the bodies scattered around on this side of the draw. One of the outlaws was such a gory mess that Longarm knew the dynamite must have exploded right next to him. Three other men were sprawled loosely in various attitudes of death, and a fifth and final man had been tied to a tree by either George or Pryor. He was whimpering in pain from the wounded arm he held closely against his body.

Given the damage done by the dynamite and the element of surprise, it was possible George and Pryor could have accounted for all the bandits on this side of the draw. But the barrage from inside the coach had certainly evened the odds. More than that, really, reflected Longarm. Mallory's men hadn't known what hit them.

"Which one's Mallory?" he asked.

"I haven't seen him," said Nola. "He must be around on the other side."

Longarm jerked his head. "Come take a look."

Nola walked around the coach beside him, and the other three women followed. Without hesitation, Nola pointed at the man who had been creased on the head. "That's him," she said, and Longarm could hear the hate in her voice. "That's Ben Mallory."

So, Longarm was finally getting a look at the man he had come here to capture. He was glad that Mallory had survived the battle. He strode over to stand above the outlaw and peered down at him. Mallory was a slender man in his thirties with dark, curly hair, not overly intelligent looking, but there was a vicious cunning in his features that matched everything Longarm knew about him. Mallory was stirring now, trying to regain consciousness, and Longarm reached down to prod him in the chest with the barrel of the Winchester.

"Wake up, Mallory," Longarm said. "It's all over. You're under arrest."

Mallory's eyes flickered open. He moved his head, then winced at the pain that must have shot through his skull. "Who . . . who are you?" he asked hoarsely.

"Deputy United States Marshal Custis Long," Longarm told him. "You're my prisoner, and I'm going to take particular pleasure in seeing you swing for murder and robbery, Mallory."

Mallory groaned and closed his eyes. They snapped open again when Nola stepped up beside Longarm and said, "Hello, Ben."

"Nola!" Mallory croaked. "I . . . I thought I saw you in that coach, but . . . I figured I was seein' things—"

"No matter how much Marshal Long enjoys seeing you hang, I'll enjoy it more, Ben," said Nola. She spat in Mallory's face, making him jerk his head to the side and groan again as he clutched his skull.

Longarm put a hand on Nola's arm and gently drew her back. "That's enough," he told her. "I reckon Mallory's figured out by now that you were working with me all along, even as muddled as he must be right now. Why don't you ladies climb back in the stage, and we'll start thinking about what we're going to do next.''

Nola gave Mallory one more venomous glance, then allowed Longarm to steer her back to the stagecoach. George and Pryor closed in on Mallory, jerked him to his feet, and tied his hands securely behind his back.

The outlaws had started their attack by shooting one of the lead horses through the head, and when it had dropped, that had forced the rest of the team and the coach to come to a halt. Once all the surviving outlaws were tied up, George and Pryor began the task of cutting the dead horse loose from its harness and backing the coach away from it. The other leader was unhitched as well and tied on behind the coach, so that the team wouldn't be unbalanced. With only four horses to pull it, the stagecoach would have to travel at a slower pace.

"We're closer to Galena City than we are to Virginia City," Longarm said. "We'll turn around and go back there, so that I can lock these owlhoots up for the time being."

"But there's no jail in Galena City," Nola pointed out. "There's not even a constable."

"Surely somebody's got a smokehouse, or a good solid storeroom," said Longarm. "That's all I'll need for now, that and somebody to stand guard."

Nola nodded. "You won't have any trouble finding volunteers for that job. Everyone in town has lived in fear of Mallory for so long, they'll all be glad to see him locked up. In fact, they'd probably be happy to take care of the trial and the execution, as well."

Longarm shook his head firmly. "There won't be any lynchings. Mallory's going to have a proper trial in Carson City."

"All right, but I imagine there'll be a good-sized delegation from Galena City to witness the hanging."

"That's fine," Longarm said. "Just as long as everything's done legal like."

With the skill of long experience, George turned the coach around to head back to Galena City. "Bat's not going to like messin' up our schedule, and neither's Claude," he warned.

"I reckon they'll both forgive us, considering we're bringing Mallory in," Longarm said. "Let's get those boys up top. The undertaker'll have to bring his wagon back out here for the dead ones . . . if the wolves have left him any customers by then."

Mallory and the other two wounded outlaws climbed awkwardly to the top of the stage. Once they were there, Pryor bound them even more tightly. "I'll keep an eye on them," he promised Longarm. He hefted the greener and added, "If they try to escape, they'll regret it."

Longarm didn't think any of the outlaws would try anything, not considering the shape they were in. Mallory was the least injured of the three, and he was still light-headed from the bullet slapping him alongside the skull.

Longarm didn't have to sit on the floor of the coach this time. He settled down on the rear seat, between Mickey and Rafaela. Nola and Angie sat facing them. Nola asked, "Are you all right, Custis? That wound of yours didn't start bleeding again, did it?"

He slipped a hand inside his shirt and checked the bandages. "Feels fine," he reported. "Still aches a little, but that's to be expected. I reckon in another week or so I'll be as good as I ever was."

Angie giggled. "And I'll bet that's mighty good. Isn't it, Nola?"

Nola just smiled coolly and said, "Some things aren't any of your business, Angie." The smile took most of the sting out of the words.

Longarm settled back against the seat, took a deep breath and blew it out in a sigh of relief. Despite the tragedies along the way—the deaths of Amelia Loftus and Mrs. Keegan—and the near-tragedies such as the bushwhackings that had resulted in Longarm and J. Emerson Dupree each catching a bullet, this job had just about come to a successful conclusion.

All he had to do now was recover the stolen silver Mallory had hidden up at that Indian burial ground . . .

# Chapter 16

Longarm ducked as a bullet chipped the rock right above his head. "Shit!" he said.

Some jobs just never turned out to be simple, no matter how much a fella hoped they would.

He was crouched among the boulders that littered the edge of a small plateau dotted with pine trees and clumps of brush. Looming above the plateau in the crystal-clear morning air was the snow-capped mountain called Virginia Peak. In the distance Longarm could see the still blue waters of Pyramid Lake extending far to the north. The plateau commanded quite a view, not as beautiful as the area around the lake called Tahoe, south of here along the California–Nevada border, but still mighty pretty. That might have had something to do with why the Paiutes had decided to lay their dead to rest here.

This was still sacred ground to the Paiutes, even though they didn't use it anymore, and they probably wouldn't have taken kindly to a bunch of white outlaws using it as a hideout. But the Paiutes had all been moved off to the reservation, and they didn't ride the warpath anymore. Chances were, none of them even knew that Mallory and his men had built a log cabin smack-dab in the middle of their sacred plateau.

"I sure wish those men Mallory left behind hadn't spotted us until we got closer," George called over to Longarm. "That cabin looks mighty solid. Who knows how long they can hold us off from in there?"

George was crouched behind another boulder about twenty feet away, and beyond him were Pryor, J. Emerson Dupree, Charlie Dodson, and half a dozen other men from Galena City and the surrounding mines. As Nola had predicted, Longarm had plenty of volunteers for anything he wanted once word got around that he had brought in Ben Mallory. George and Pryor had asked to come along because they worked for the California & Nevada Stage Line; Dupree was here because he wanted the story of the remaining outlaws' capture; and Dodson and the other men just wanted to be in on the finish. They had all ridden up here this morning because the stagecoach had gotten back into Galena City too late on the previous afternoon to start then.

Unfortunately, the men Mallory had left behind to guard the loot from earlier robberies had to be suspicious because their leader and the rest of the gang hadn't returned when they were supposed to. Mallory wouldn't be coming back. He was locked up in Galena City, along with the other two surviving outlaws.

Longarm and his unofficial posse had tried to cover the open ground surrounding the cabin without being seen, but the men inside had spotted them and opened fire, driving them back to cover in the rocks at the edge of the plateau. Since then it had been a standoff. The outlaws couldn't get out of the cabin, but Longarm and his companions were pinned down here in these boulders.

There had to be some way to shake those owlhoots out of their hole, thought Longarm. He just hadn't been able to come up with it yet.

At least he didn't have to worry about Nola and the other women during this fight, he reminded himself. They were safely back in Galena City.

He reached into his shirt pocket and took out a cheroot.

135

As he clamped it between his teeth, it reminded him of something, and without pausing to light the cigar, he stuck his hand in the pocket of the sheepskin jacket. Sure enough, the two sticks of dynamite he had put in there the day before, following the gunfight with Mallory's gang, were still there.

Longarm grinned around the cheroot as he called to the other men, "Who's got the strongest arm?"

"That might be me," said George with a frown. "Wrestlin' with those stagecoach teams builds up a fella's muscles."

Longarm flipped one of the sticks of dynamite across the gap between his cover and the boulder where George was crouched. "Think you could heave that all the way to the cabin?" he asked.

George caught the dynamite, but he looked plenty nervous as he did so. "Good Lord, Marshal!" he exclaimed. "You can't just go tossing this stuff around like that. It goes off if you look at it wrong!"

"I reckon it's safe enough if you're careful," said Longarm. "Just be sure you're ready to throw it before you light the fuse."

Pryor volunteered, "I'll do it if you don't want to, George."

"No, that's all right," grumbled George. He patted the pockets of his coat. "Lemme find a match."

A few moments later, Longarm caught a whiff of sulphur in the mountain air as George lit a match and held it to the fuse. As soon as the fuse caught, George dropped the match and quickly drew back his arm. He rose up slightly to throw the dynamite toward the outlaws' cabin.

A rifle cracked from inside the cabin, and the bullet drilled into George's shoulder, knocking him backward. The dynamite slipped from his hand and bounced a couple of feet down the slope. George landed where he could see the fuse hissing and sputtering, and he let out a yell of sheer terror.

Longarm bolted out from behind the boulder and launched himself in a long, desperate dive toward George and the dynamite. "Hit the dirt!" he yelled to the other men. The fingers of his outstretched hand closed around the cylinder and flipped it away as Longarm crashed into the ground.

The dynamite spun up into the air and exploded.

The force of the blast drove Longarm's head against the rocky slope, and for a second he couldn't see anything except a dizzy blackness shot through with streaks of red. Then his vision cleared and his hearing began to come back. He saw George lying nearby, clutching a wounded shoulder. George's mouth was moving, and gradually Longarm began to hear the profanity spewing from the jehu's lips.

Longarm grinned despite the pain in his side. That had been a close one.

He pushed himself onto hands and knees, grabbed George, and pulled him into a more secure position behind the boulder. George's wound was painful but not too serious, Longarm decided. A glance along the rim of the plateau told him that the other men were shaken but all right. Charlie Dodson called, "Got any more of that dynamite, Marshal?"

"One more stick," replied Longarm as he reached into his jacket pocket where he had tucked away the other red-wrapped cylinder. He brought it out, tossed it over to Pryor, who passed it on to Dodson. Longarm asked the mine superintendent, "Can you reach the cabin with it?"

"I swung a sledgehammer and a pickax for a long time before I started pushing papers," said Dodson. "I'll give it a try."

Longarm picked up George's rifle. His own Winchester was back there behind the boulder he had been using for cover before. "Let's give him some covering fire, boys," Longarm called to the other men. He stuck the barrel of the rifle over the top of the boulder and started blazing away. Pryor and the other men followed his lead, pouring their fire toward the cabin.

Dodson lit the fuse, stood up, and heaved the dynamite toward the cabin as hard as he could. Longarm yelled, "Hold

137

your fire!'' He didn't want a stray bullet setting off the dynamite before it got there.

The outlaws forted up in the cabin must have heard the blast from the first stick, thought Longarm, and they had to suspect that the posse would try again. They opened up from inside the cabin, attempting to set off the dynamite before it reached its target. The cylinder kept spinning through the air, though, untouched by the rifle fire, trailing the sparking fuse. It hit the ground about fifteen feet from the cabin wall, bounced twice, and rolled to a stop only inches from the wall just as the fuse burned down.

The explosion sent logs flying into the air. When the dust and smoke cleared, Longarm saw that a hole had been blasted into the side of the cabin, and the whole structure was leaning crazily now. The roof began to collapse with a grinding and crashing sound. Through the jagged hole in the wall, Longarm saw movement, and a second later three men stumbled out of the collapsing cabin. One of them was dressed only in tattered, bloodstained shreds of clothing. He must have been right on the other side of the wall from where the dynamite had gone off, thought Longarm.

All three of the outlaws were empty-handed. "Enough!" one of them shouted between shuddering coughs. "We give up, damn it! Don't shoot!"

Longarm and the other members of the posse came out on the flat top of the plateau and kept their guns trained on the outlaws as they advanced toward the wrecked cabin. In a matter of moments, the three men Mallory had left behind to guard the hideout had their hands tied securely behind their backs.

Longarm, Dodson, and Dupree walked over to the cabin while Pryor and the other men herded the prisoners toward the edge of the plateau. Longarm peered into the ruins and saw a couple of trunks sitting next to some crude cots that had been overturned by the force of the blast. The trunks weren't locked. Longarm stepped carefully through the debris and reached the nearest trunk. He lifted the lid.

Silver ingots gleamed dully in the sunlight.

"Incredible," said Dupree. "There's a small fortune here. What was Mallory going to do with it?"

"I expect when he figured he had enough, he'd pack it all out and head for San Francisco or someplace like that," said Longarm. "His share would have been enough to let him live like a king for a long time."

"There's plenty here for that already," Dodson pointed out.

Longarm shrugged. "Outlaws are generally greedier than they are smart. That's what trips 'em up." He winced as he felt the sticky wetness on his side. "Damn. Must've busted those bullet holes open again when I went diving after that stick of dynamite."

Dodson slapped him heartily on the shoulder. "We'll patch you up, Marshal, and ol' George, too. I reckon that'll do until we can get you back to Galena City." The mine superintendent grinned broadly. "And once you're back in the hands of Miss Sutton and her ladies, I'm sure they'll take mighty good care of you."

Longarm had to grin, too. This time, he was looking forward to recuperating in the Silver Slipper.


"All that work getting you healthy again," Nola said crossly, "and you go and ruin it, Custis."

"Couldn't let George get his head blowed off," Longarm explained patiently. "Not if I could help it."

Rafaela pulled a fresh bandage tight around his midsection. "You could have been killed, too, you know," she said.

Longarm inclined his head in acknowledgment of her point. "True enough, but that happens all the time in my line of work. Seems like not a month goes by when somebody's not doing their damnedest to kill me."

"I couldn't live like that," said Angie. "I'd be afraid all the time."

Mickey stroked Longarm's bare shoulder. "Custis is not afraid," she said. "Custis is a brave man."

139

He grinned at the four women standing around him as he sat in Nola's room. "Custis is a damned lucky man," he said, "to have four ladies like you looking after him."

"Yes, well, one of these days we're liable to get tired of patching you up," Nola said. Her expression softened slightly. "I'm just glad you captured Mallory and recovered all that silver."

Rafaela was finished with her bandaging, so Longarm leaned back and sighed. "Might never have been able to do it without the four of you," he said solemnly. "You've got my thanks, and the thanks of the Justice Department."

"That and two bits will buy a drink," said Nola. Longarm could tell she was somewhat uncomfortable with his gratitude, so he decided not to press the issue.

Instead, he said, "It's been a long day. I could use something to eat."

"And then some rest," Nola said. Longarm nodded in agreement.

It had taken a while to do a rough job of doctoring on Longarm and George, as well as to figure out a way to haul all that silver back to Galena City. The posse had wound up unloading the silver and splitting it up among them, leaving the trunks in the ruined cabin. All the saddlebags on the posse's horses had been stuffed full, but the silver was now safe and sound, locked up in the stagecoach station. With Mallory now in custody, Charlie Dodson and the other mine superintendents planned to send wagons into town the next day to load up the silver and take it to Carson City.

Evening was fast approaching as Longarm and Nola shared a meal in her bedroom. Longarm felt himself getting drowsy. Even though it was only dusk outside, when he was finished eating, he yawned and said, "I reckon I'm going to have to turn in."

"You go right ahead, Custis," Nola told him. "Like I said before, you need your rest."

Longarm couldn't argue with that. Nola pulled the curtains

closed as he climbed into bed, and then she blew out the lamp before slipping quietly from the room.

A deep, dreamless sleep claimed Longarm, and he had no idea how much time had passed when he suddenly awoke. His lawman's instincts had alerted him to something, and as he rolled over quickly, he discovered what it was.

A naked woman had climbed into bed with him.

She put her arms around him and kissed him, her lips unerringly finding his, even in the dimness of the room. His arms went around her, and he expected to feel Nola's familiar contours. Instead, he was surprised to realize that the woman snuggling against him was considerably more slender and less endowed than Nola.

"Rafaela?" he whispered.

"Ssshhh." Her fingers wrapped hotly around his hardening shaft. "Just lie still, Custis."

His visitor was Rafaela, all right. He was lying on his side, and after a moment she turned so that she was lying next to him, spoon-fashion, with her rear nestled against his groin. His rigid manhood slipped between her thighs and rubbed against the lightly furred lips of her femininity. She moved her hips back and forth, creating a delicious friction even though he had not yet penetrated her. Longarm slipped his arms around her so that he could fondle her small, pear-shaped breasts.

The door of the room made a slight noise as it opened and closed.

Longarm caught his breath, not knowing what to expect as a figure darted across the shadows of the room. He would have rolled away from Rafaela and reached for his gun on the bedside table, but she clamped her thighs together tightly, holding him in place. "It's all right," she said.

A second later, Longarm heard the whisper of silk, and then the bed sank a little behind him as someone else climbed in. Soft lips kissed the back of his neck as long hair slid enticingly over his shoulder. He felt another nude woman pressing herself against him from behind. It was a little more

141

difficult for him to be sure, but he didn't think this was Nola, either, and his second mysterious visitor wasn't big enough to be Angie. That left Mickey.

"We make Custis happy," she whispered in his ear, confirming his guess. One of her hands boldly explored his body, stealing between his legs from behind to cup and caress his sac.

He groaned in pleasure. "Damn right you make Custis happy," he said hoarsely. He moved his upper arm and reached back so that he could caress Mickey's hip. She arched against him.

This was what the old saying about an embarrassment of riches must mean, Longarm thought as he nuzzled the side of Rafaela's neck. It had been a while since he had been in bed with two women at the same time, but he hadn't forgotten what a special pleasure it was. He explored and caressed Rafaela, searching out all her secret places, while Mickey did the same to him.

"Be . . . careful . . . Custis," Rafaela gasped out, breathless with joy. "You don't want to . . . hurt yourself again."

"You ladies are the best medicine I know," Longarm said as he boldly slipped a finger into Rafaela's womanhood. She caught hold of his hand and pressed him deeper into her.

Somehow, Longarm wasn't surprised when the door opened again.

"Is it all right to come in now?" asked Angie as she leaned in from the hallway.

Longarm had to laugh. "Come on in," he called. He stopped himself from saying "The more, the merrier." But he thought it.

Angie stepped into the room, closed the door behind her, and hurried over to the bed. In the brief flash of light from the corridor, Longarm saw that she was already nude, and spectacularly nude at that. Her bountiful breasts were tipped with large circles of pale pink, and the triangle of hair at the juncture of her thighs was thick and blond. She climbed onto the bed from the foot of it and straddled Longarm's calves

142

as Mickey and Rafaela urged him to roll over onto his back. His manhood, hard as a bar of steel when it was released from the glorious trap of Rafaela's thighs, sprang up into the air. Angie leaned forward and wrapped both hands around it.

"Damn, Custis," she said. "I never saw a pecker quite so nice before."

Longarm would have thanked her for the compliment, but before he could say anything, she leaned forward even more and took the head of his shaft into her mouth. Her lips closed around it tightly, and she began to suck greedily.

He started to moan, but Mickey stopped that by kissing him. Her tongue darted into his mouth. At the same time, Rafaela began running her fingers through the thick mat of hair on his chest and tonguing his nipples, each in turn. Longarm put his left arm around Mickey and his right around Rafaela.

When Mickey finally took her mouth away from his, he gasped for air, then said, "Does Nola know about this?"

"It was her idea," murmured Rafaela. She moved her head lower on his belly, trailing kisses that set his senses on fire. When she reached his groin, she told Angie, "My turn now."

Grudgingly, Angie relinquished the thick pole of male flesh and straightened as Rafaela opened her mouth and engulfed it. Mickey was moving in that direction, too, and Longarm threw his head back on the pillows and thought, *Oh, Lord, they're going to take turns!*

That was exactly what they did, first one and then the other and then the third one sucking and licking and kissing until Longarm thought that he was going to explode. He wasn't just thinking of his manhood, either, he realized. It felt as if his entire body was about to fly apart at the seams.

Finally, Rafaela lifted her lips from him and said, "I don't think he's going to last much longer. You'd better go ahead, Angie."

"You reckon it'll be all right?" asked Angie.

143

"Go on," Mickey urged her.

*Good grief*, thought Longarm. They had worked all this out among themselves ahead of time. Obviously, Angie was going to have the honor of bringing him to a climax. Well, that wasn't going to take a hell of a lot of work, he told himself.

Still straddling him, she moved up so that she was poised above his hips. She reached down and gripped his shaft to guide it into its natural slot, which was hot and slick with wetness. She was surprisingly tight, confirming Longarm's suspicion that she hadn't been in her current line of work for very long. She slid down onto him until he was completely buried inside her. She gasped in ecstasy as the head of his shaft hit bottom.

"Oh, Custis, you fill me up so good!" she moaned.

Her hips began to pump back and forth as she rode him. Longarm reached up and caught hold of her breasts, his fingers sinking into the soft flesh as he cupped and kneaded them. Rafaela and Mickey sprawled on either side of him, nipping and kissing at his chest, shoulders, and neck.

Just as Rafaela had predicted, he didn't last very long. He had let Angie do most of the work, but as he felt his seed boiling up he gripped her hips and held her still as he drove into her, bottoming out again and holding it there. He began to spasm, the hot, thick juices exploding out of him and flooding into her. Rafaela and Mickey threw their arms around him and hung on. Angie cried out as her own climax shook her. Longarm shuddered once, twice, three times as the last of his seed leaped from him. He fell back against the pillows.

"Are you sure . . . you gals . . . ain't trying to kill me?" he asked when he could summon up enough breath to speak again.

Angie leaned over and kissed him quickly, almost shyly. "Oh, Custis, that was so good," she whispered. "I wish you could do that to me every day for the rest of my life."

He reached up and stroked her hair. "That'd be a mighty

144

nice way to spend the next forty years or so," he said. "If I didn't have a job waiting for me, that is."

Rafaela and Mickey each kissed him on the cheek. "You are a nice man, Custis Long," whispered Rafaela. She almost sounded sad about something, Longarm thought, but then, Rafaela was always more solemn than the other young women.

"Nola will be here later," Rafaela went on. "She said that you were to sleep when we were finished with you."

"Sounds good to me," said Longarm with a drowsy grin. "You ladies wrung me out, that's for damn sure."

The three of them slipped out of the bed. Angie was the most reluctant to go. She leaned over and gave his now-soft manhood a farewell squeeze. "When do you reckon you'll be ready to go again?" she asked.

"Angie," Rafaela said sternly before Longarm could answer. "Come along now. Remember what Nola said."

"Yeah, I guess you're right." She grinned brightly at Longarm. "Good night, Custis!"

"Good night, Angie," he told her. "Good night to all you ladies."

The three women slipped out of the room, and Longarm rolled onto his right side again, favoring the left side where he had been shot. Even after all the exertion of the last hour or so, the wound didn't feel too bad, and it hadn't started bleeding again. He chuckled as he thought of the way those three hussies had taken advantage of a poor, injured man.

As he drifted off to sleep, he wondered if they might be willing to take advantage of him again a few more times before he started back to Denver.

# Chapter 17

He woke up to the sound of a metallic clicking.

Thinking that someone in the room had just cocked a gun, Longarm started to lunge upright in the bed. His hand reached out for the pistol on the table.

His arm was jerked back before it got there, and he was thrown back down on the pillows. "What the hell!" he exclaimed.

"I'm sorry, Custis, I truly am. But I just can't pass this chance up. There may never be another one."

That was Nola's voice. Longarm looked up, saw her in the light of the lamp that was burning on the dressing table. Something clattered, and he looked down at his hands.

A pair of manacles had been snapped around his wrists, and they were attached to a chain that was fastened around one of the bedposts.

"What the hell!" Longarm said again, this time practically in a roar.

"Just settle down, Custis, and no one will get hurt," said Nola. Her voice was calm, yet it had a faint quaver in it.

Longarm stared at her in astonishment. She was wearing boots, denim trousers, and a man's shirt and jacket. Her hair was tucked up under a broad-brimmed Stetson. She even had a gunbelt buckled around her trim hips. With her red hair and the way she was dressed, she reminded Longarm of his old friend Jessie Starbuck, but Jessie was 'way down in Texas and had always been on the side of the law.

From the looks of things, Nola had decided to try the outlaw trail. Either that, or she had something mighty odd in mind for pleasuring herself with him.

Longarm forced his raging emotions to settle down, just as Nola had urged. He said in a fairly calm voice, "All right, Nola, what's this all about?"

"It ought to be obvious, Custis," she replied. "You're my prisoner."

"What are you going to do to me?" he asked, a part of him still hoping that this might be just some sort of game.

"I'm not going to do anything to you. I like you, Custis, and I don't want to see you hurt. That's why I'm going to leave you locked up here in my room, so that no harm will come to you when I take that silver and leave town with it."

"Son of a bitch!" exploded Longarm. He had been afraid Nola was going to say something like that. She was dressed for traveling in a hurry, and that meant a getaway of some sort. That pile of recovered loot was about the only thing in Galena City worth getting away with.

"I know you thought better of me than that, and I'm truly sorry to disappoint you, Custis," Nola went on. "But let's face it—I'm a whore, and if money wasn't important to me, I wouldn't be in this line of work."

He gestured as much as he could with his chained hands. "What about the Silver Slipper? Looks to me like it makes plenty of money!"

"The place is profitable," admitted Nola. "But I could run this saloon for the rest of my life and not make as much as what's sitting over there in that stage station." She shook her head. "No, I have to do this. All my life I've wanted to be so rich that nobody could ever hurt me again. Ever since I was twelve years old and my brothers started taking turns with me on the farm back in Iowa—"

She stopped short, taking a deep, ragged breath. "But that

147

doesn't matter to you, does it, Custis? You carry a badge, so when you get right down to it, nothing matters to you except the law."

That wasn't strictly true, thought Longarm. He had bent the rules on more than one occasion to see justice done. But Nola wouldn't understand that, any more than he could really understand the pain inside her that had to be driving her.

He lifted his manacled hands. "Take these things off me, Nola, and we'll just forget that this ever happened. Hell, everybody gets carried away now and then—"

She shook her head and put her hand on the butt of the gun on her hip. "I can't do that."

"I reckon I understand now why you worked so hard to keep me alive," Longarm said, letting some of the bitterness he felt come out in his voice. "You had to keep me healthy until I recovered that silver."

"That . . . wasn't the only reason," said Nola. "Remember, at first I didn't even know why you were here."

That was true, and Longarm had to admit it. When he had stumbled into her office downstairs with a bullet hole in his side, she had risked her life to save him from Mallory's men, and at the time she'd had no idea there might be something in it for her. Still, that didn't justify what she was doing now.

"You're going to have to kill me to keep me from coming after you," he said. "You know that, don't you?"

"Like I said, no one's going to get hurt." She turned to the door and swung it open. "Come on in, girls."

Longarm wasn't surprised to see Angie, Mickey, and Rafaela file into the room. Nor was he surprised by their garb. Instead of the gaudy outfits they wore on the dance floor of the saloon, they were dressed in range clothes like Nola, complete with boots, hats, and guns. With the bulky jackets they wore, they could have been taken for men instead of women, especially on a dark night.

"So all of you were in it together," said Longarm. "That's why the three of you came to see me earlier. You felt guilty because of what you were planning, so you figured

148

a little slap-and-tickle would make it all right."

"You shouldn't talk to us like that, Custis," said Angie. Of the four women, she was the only one who looked truly regretful. "We like you, we really do. But that silver is worth *so* much money . . ."

Stubbornly, he shook his head. "I ain't going to tell you that what you're doing is all right. I just can't."

"Well, we're doing it anyway, whether you approve or not." Nola gestured toward the bed. "Let's finish it up."

Longarm opened his mouth to yell for help, but before any sound could come from his mouth, Angie bounded across the room and clapped her hand over his lips. She wrapped her other arm around his shoulders and bore him down on the bed. Longarm tried to kick his feet as one of the other women grabbed them, but a cord was wrapped around his ankles with the speed and dexterity of a cowboy tying the legs of a calf with a piggin' string. Another rope ran from his ankles to one of the posts at the foot of the bed. Angie lifted her hand from his mouth, and Nola was ready to shove a wadded-up piece of cloth between his lips. Longarm tried to spit it out, but another strip of cloth was whipped around his head and tied to make the gag secure. He couldn't yell, he was bound hand and foot, and he was naked except for the bandages around his middle.

This was a damned sorry state of affairs, he thought.

If he had been at full strength, they might not have been able to do such things to him. But he was already somewhat weakened from everything he had gone through during the past week or so, and the bout of lovemaking with Angie and Rafaela and Mickey had worn him out even more. He had fallen into such a deep, exhausted sleep that Nola had been able to slip the manacles onto him without waking him, and now he had been unable to summon up the energy to throw off the other women as they finished the job of trussing him up. Longarm was thoroughly disgusted with himself.

The women straightened from their work and stepped back from the bed. Nola looked Longarm over and nodded in satisfaction. "I've left a note downstairs for my head bar-tender," she told him. "He'll find it tomorrow morning and turn you loose. You'll be all right until then. And by then, we'll be a long way from Galena City."

Longarm grunted angrily around the gag. That was all he could do.

Nola jerked her head toward the door and said, "Let's go."

Angie lifted a hand and wiggled her fingers. "Goodbye, Custis."

Rafaela and Mickey said their goodbyes as well, and at least they had the good grace to look a little embarrassed by the whole thing, Longarm noted. They slipped out of the room along with Angie, leaving Nola alone with him.

"You're the best man I've ever met, Custis, and I mean that in more ways than one," she said. "It's too bad you didn't come along a few years earlier."

Longarm made some more muffled gruntings.

"I wish things were different, too," said Nola, "but they're not. Goodbye, Custis."

Longarm would have cursed if he had been able to. As it was, all he could do was glare as Nola left the room and closed the door softly behind her.

Then he was alone, with nothing but his own anger and frustration to keep him company.

The soft knocking roused Claude Jessup from his sleep on the cot in the back room of the stage station. He hadn't been about to just go off and leave all that silver unguarded, so he had decided to sleep here with his shotgun at his side. George and Pryor had offered to stay with him, but he had sent them on down to the hotel to get some rest. "I'll be fine," Jessup had told them.

Now, as he was pulled from sleep in the middle of the night, he had to wonder who was knocking on the door. It couldn't be anybody trying to steal the silver, he told himself.

Thieves would have just busted down the door, instead of knocking.

Jessup had been sleeping in his pants and long underwear. As he stood up, he pulled his suspenders up onto his shoulders, then reached down and picked up the shotgun. He padded into the front room of the station and went to the door. "Who is it?" he called, standing to one side of the door just in case anybody tried to shoot through it.

A woman's voice replied, startling him. He had expected to hear a man. "It's Nola Sutton, Claude. I need to talk to you."

Jessup hesitated, despite the fact that he liked Nola and found himself very attracted to her. "What's this about?" he asked.

"Marshal Long sent me over here with a message for you. He said it was urgent."

Well, that was different, Jessup supposed. Everybody in town knew by now that Nola and the lawman were close. After all, she had hidden him out when Mallory's men were searching for him and had nursed him back to health from that gunshot wound.

"Hang on a minute," he called through the door. "I'll light a lamp."

He set the shotgun aside and fumbled a match from his pants pocket. A moment later, he had the lamp lit on his desk, and the yellow glow filled the room, illuminating the stack of mailbags in the corner that were filled with silver ingots. The California & Nevada Stage Line was going to loan the bags to the mines so that the silver could be transported to Carson City in them.

Jessup went back to the door without bothering to pick up his shotgun. He took the key from his pocket, thrust it in the lock, turned it. He rattled the knob and swung the door open. "What's the message from Marshal L—" he began.

The words choked off abruptly when he saw the muzzle of the gun pointing straight at his face.

"Step back, Claude," said Nola Sutton as she looked at

151

him over the barrel of the pistol. "I don't want to have to hurt you."

Without moving his head, Jessup darted his eyes toward the shotgun, which was leaning against a table a few feet away. Nola saw the look and said, "I wish you wouldn't, Claude. I'll put a bullet through your head before you can ever reach it."

Jessup sighed. "I made a bad mistake, didn't I?"

"I'm afraid so. Now back up, away from the door."

With another sigh, Jessup stepped back. Nola followed, keeping the pistol trained on him. Jessup got another surprise when he saw how she was dressed. Three more women whom he recognized from the Silver Slipper crowded into the room behind Nola. All of them were dressed more like cowboys than saloon girls.

"Get the shotgun," Nola said, and one of the women picked it up. The other two came toward Claude, veering to the sides so they could go around him. One of them was the big blond called Angie, and she was the one who grabbed his arms and jerked them behind his back. She held him while the other one tied him up.

With her foot, Nola pushed a chair over to him. "You might as well sit down, Claude," she said. "You're going to be here for a while."

Jessup sank onto the chair, and moving quickly, the women lashed him to it, even tying his ankles to the legs of the chair. "I'm liable to lose my job because of this," he said sadly.

"I'm sorry, but it can't be helped. That silver is going with us."

"What about Marshal Long? Did you kill him?"

Nola looked genuinely offended at the question, and Angie exclaimed, "Of course we didn't kill him! What do you think we are?"

"Thieves," said Jessup bitterly. "Thieves and whores."

Nola's lips curved in a thin smile. "That's absolutely right, Claude. But we're not killers. Not unless someone

152

forces us to be." She holstered her gun now that he was tied securely. "Go ahead and gag him."

Jessup made it difficult for them, jerking his head from side to side. The way he was tied up, that was the only part of him that could still move. But then Angie grabbed his jaw and held him still while one of the other women forced a gag into his mouth and tied it in place.

" All right, let's take the silver out the back," Nola said.

Jessup sat and watched helplessly as they picked up the mailbags and carried them out the rear door of the stage station. They left the door open, letting in cold air and the noises of a team of horses shifting around and stamping their feet. The women had a wagon back there, Jessup realized. They would need a wagon to transport such a heavy load of silver.

Nola stepped back into the building long enough to say, "Goodbye, Claude. I'm sorry we never got the chance to know each other better. You should have spoken up and asked for what you wanted when you came into the Silver Slipper. That's the only way you ever get anything in this world, you know."

Then she was gone, closing the door softly behind her.

Jessup wasn't sure how long he sat there fuming. Finally, he lifted his gaze to the table where the lamp was still burning. His eyes widened as an idea occurred to him, and he began pushing with his feet, working the chair across the planks of the floor, inch by scraping inch. His bonds were so tight that his progress was maddeningly slow.

But gradually he drew closer and closer to the table. He was taking a chance, but he had to do *something*. If he just sat here and waited for someone to come along and untie him, those women would likely be long gone by the time he was discovered. Bat Thompson would fire him, and he would be a laughingstock.

Jessup wasn't going to let that happen if he could help it. When he was close enough, he tensed his muscles, gathering himself for the effort, and then threw himself forward, chair

153

and all. He slammed into the table and sent it skidding several feet. Jessup toppled to the floor.

The lamp, knocked off the table by the impact, crashed to the floor a second later, shattering. The kerosene in its reservoir splattered and then caught fire. Flames danced up brightly as they started to spread. Jessup scooted as far away from them as he could.

Now, all he could do was hope that someone would spot the flames and come running to put out the fire . . . before he burned to death.

# Chapter 18

Longarm let himself brood, for about five minutes, over what Nola and the others had done to him, then he got busy trying to figure out a way to get loose.

The chain looped around the bedpost would slide up and down a short distance, but the post flared out enough at the top to prevent the chain from coming off of it. The post was all one piece, too, unlike some that screwed down into the bedframe.

If he could get his feet loose, he might be able to twist around and kick the wall until someone came to investigate the noise. That was a possibility worth investigating. He stretched his arms toward his feet, trying to see if he could reach the knots of the ropes around his ankles.

The chain attached to the manacles wouldn't stretch anywhere near far enough, he discovered, and he couldn't draw his legs up and bring his feet closer because of the rope that ran from them to one of the posts at the foot of the bed. With that idea eliminated, he tried to get his hands on the knot at the back of his head so that he could get rid of the gag and start yelling. That didn't work, either. There wasn't quite enough play in the chain, no matter how much he twisted his head and strained. He flopped back on the bed, a little breathless from his efforts.

Nola had planned well. He had known she was intelligent, but he had never expected her to pull something like this. If she could fool Claude Jessup as well as she had fooled him, then the silver was as good as hers. And Longarm had a feeling Jessup would be even less of a match for Nola's cunning than he had been.

When he had recovered a little, he tried a new tack. Longarm grasped what little slack there was in the chain and pulled, lifting himself up off the bed as both the chain and the rope tightened. He only came up an inch or so, but when he took up that slack and pulled again, he rose a little higher. The rope at his feet became even more taut. Slowly, Longarm repeated the process.

This was sort of like how the old *padres* in the Spanish Inquisition had stretched fellas on the rack, he thought as he tried to ignore the pain in his legs and ankles. It was a matter of what was going to give first: the rope, the bedpost . . . or his bones and muscles. The rope was a good strong one, and he didn't hold out much hope of it breaking. Those posts at the foot of the bed were thinner than the ones at the head, though. There was a slight chance . . . not much of one, though . . .

But it was the only one he had right now.

The post was flared and curved like the others, and as Longarm heaved on the chain, the rope suddenly slipped upward a little. Only a fraction of an inch, but even that much was a blessed relief. Longarm was hanging between the posts with his weight completely off the bed now, and his arms and shoulders were beginning to ache and burn like fire. His side hurt, too, and he thought he felt a trickle of wetness underneath the bandages. The bullet wound had probably broken open again.

Longarm jerked with his feet, trying to slide the knotted rope farther up the post. The higher the rope was, the better the chance he could break the post. He knew that much about forces and angles, even though he didn't have an engineering degree like that El Aguila fella he knew down in Texas who

156

rode for the Rangers. He pulled on the chain and lifted himself again, then began trying to draw his legs up. The first effort didn't accomplish anything except to send fresh stabs of pain shooting through him.

*Catch your breath and try again, old son.* He repeated that litany to himself over and over as he strained against the rope. Finally, after God only knew how many tries he had made, Longarm was rewarded with a faint cracking sound. Encouraged, he tightened his grip on the chain and pulled again with his legs, and again he heard the cracking noise.

That was either the bedpost or his leg bones. At the moment, Longarm didn't really want to know which. He pulled again.

The bedpost snapped.

The sudden loss of tension dropped Longarm back on the bed. He yelled against the gag as pain coursed through him, not only from his side but also from his legs and arms and shoulders. The strain on his entire body had been terrific, and not very many men could have done such a thing. Only the fires of determination inside Longarm had kept him going.

He lay there for long moments, waiting for the agony to subside, breathing heavily through his nose since he couldn't gasp for air around the gag. Finally, when he felt strong enough, he drew his legs up, pulling the broken bedpost with them. By bending almost double, he could reach his ankles now, and he began tugging at the ropes that bound his ankles together.

The knots had been pulled even tighter by his efforts to escape, and he struggled with them for long minutes, breaking fingernails and scraping the tips of his fingers raw against the rope. He felt the bonds loosen slightly and redoubled his efforts. One by one the knots gave, and at last the ropes fell away from his feet.

That was when he discovered that his feet had gone completely numb. Pins and needles seemed to gouge his flesh as the blood flow resumed.

With his legs free, Longarm twisted around and pushed

himself up onto his knees. He tried lifting the manacle chain off the bedpost, but as he had suspected, the post was too thick to allow the loop in the chain to pass over it. He pushed himself higher, creating more slack in the chain. Now he could reach the gag and rip it out of his mouth. He started yelling hoarsely as well as kicking the wall. Someone was bound to hear the commotion.

Sure enough, after about five minutes of hollering and pounding, a tentative knock sounded on the door. "You all right in there, Marshal Long?" someone called.

Longarm recognized the voice. It belonged to one of the bartenders from downstairs. "Get in here!" he bellowed. "Now!"

The door opened, and the man stuck his head into the room without coming any farther. His eyes widened when he saw Longarm crouched on the bed, his hands chained and blood seeping through the bandages that were his only garment.

It was embarrassing as all hell, but Longarm didn't have time to feel ashamed now. He shook the manacles at the bartender and said, "Have you got a key for these?"

"Ah . . . I don't know," the man replied. "I can go downstairs and look around . . ."

"Get over here," snapped Longarm. "Take my gun out of its holster and shoot that padlock off the chain."

"I . . . I don't know if I can do that."

"Damn it, I'm a federal lawman!" Longarm roared. "If you don't want to wind up behind bars, you'll do what I told you."

By this time, more people were starting to gather in the hall. Longarm heard a few titters of laughter as they looked past the bartender and saw his predicament. He gritted his teeth. Nola was going to be sorry for more than stealing that silver, he vowed. She would pay for leaving him in this ridiculous position.

The bartender was still hesitating, and Longarm was about to yell at him again when a deep voice said, "What the hell is all this?'' Charlie Dodson shouldered his way into the room, followed by J. Emerson Dupree.

Longarm closed his eyes and tried not to groan. He was glad to see Dodson, but the presence of the newspaperman made him worry about what the headlines might be in the next edition of the Galena City *Bugle*.

*Mine Superintendent Rescues Naked Lawman in Chains.*

Longarm shook his head to drive that thought away, then said, "Charlie, blow that lock off, would you?"

"Sure." Dodson drew his own gun. Longarm could tell that he was trying not to grin. "Get a little carried away with your foolin' around, did you?"

"Fooling around, hell!" said Longarm. "Nola Sutton and three of her girls have probably stolen that load of silver by now!"

Dodson's eyes got big with surprise. "The devil you say!" he exclaimed. He thrust out his pistol, aimed, and fired twice, shattering the lock that held the chain to the bed. The chain dropped away, leaving Longarm free at last to move around, even though his wrists were still manacled.

He grabbed his pants and pulled them on awkwardly, then said to Dodson and Dupree, "We'd better get over to the stage station."

Dupree gestured at the bloodstained bandages. "You're injured again, Marshal."

"No time for that," said Longarm. "Come on."

He practically ran out of the room, gathering up the chain so that it wouldn't trip him. Dodson got folks out of the way, and the three of them hurried downstairs and out onto Comstock Street. Longarm peered down Greenwood Avenue toward the stage station. Nothing appeared to be out of the ordinary . . .

That was when he spotted the leaping red and yellow glow inside the building.

"Fire!" he shouted. "The stage station is on fire!"

Longarm, Dodson, and Dupree were in the lead, but a large group of people followed them down Greenwood Avenue as they ran toward the stagecoach station. Longarm was barefoot and nude from the waist up except for the bandages, but he didn't notice the cold. Why would Nola have set the stage station on fire before leaving, he asked himself, or was she not to blame for the blaze? Who else could have started it?

He got his answer a few minutes later. Charlie Dodson kicked open the door and plunged into the burning building while some of the other citizens began forming a bucket brigade from the town well. A moment later Dodson dragged a bulky, odd-looking form out of the station. As the flames grew larger and cast a garish illumination into the street, Longarm realized that he was looking at Claude Jessup. The stationkeeper had been tied to a straight-backed chair. Dodson took out his knife and slashed the ropes binding Jessup to the chair, then helped him to his feet. Jessup looked plenty shaken. With fumbling fingers, he pulled a gag from his mouth.

"It . . . it was Miss Sutton!" he said. "Her and some of her girls! They stole that silver—"

"Did they start the fire?" asked Longarm.

Jessup shook his head. "I did that. Knocked over a lamp. I was hoping somebody would see the fire and come a-runnin'. Thank God you did and got here in time."

But not in time to save the building, thought Longarm as he glanced at the stage station. With luck, the bucket brigade would be able to keep the fire from spreading, though. They were already wetting down the surrounding structures, including the barn in the back.

Longarm lifted his wrists. "I've got to get these manacles off so that I can go after 'em," he said.

"If you can't find the key, I reckon the blacksmith can bust 'em off of you," said Dodson.

"And you'd better have that wound seen to, as well," added Dupree.

Longarm was tempted to once again say that there was no time for that, but he knew Dupree was right. He couldn't

160

afford to pass out from loss of blood. Nola and the other women had a head start, but not a huge one by any means. And they would have to be traveling fairly slowly, too, whether they were carrying the silver in a wagon or on horseback. Longarm thought a wagon was the most likely possibility.

Jessup confirmed that. "It sounded to me like they headed north out of town," he went on. "That would be the easiest route, once they hit the Truckee River and could turn east or west."

"I'll find 'em, you can count on that," promised Longarm.

"Looks like you'll need a posse again," commented Dodson.

Longarm shook his head. "Not this time. I can travel faster alone." His voice grew more grim as he added, "And this time they sure as hell won't take me by surprise."

Ben Mallory stood near the back of the cold, dank cellar as the trapdoor leading to the house above was opened. One of the guards tossed down a burlap sack. "There's some food in there," the man called.

One of the other outlaws whined, "When are we goin' to get out of here? This cold and damp is makin' my rheumatiz act up somethin' terrible."

"You should have thought of that before you took up the profession of banditry, my friend," called the guard. He was the young shotgunner from the stagecoach, Mallory realized. He was the one who talked so fancy.

The trapdoor fell with a thump, and Mallory heard the bolts being shot to fasten it. He and the other five members of the gang who had survived had been dumped unceremoniously in here to wait until they could be taken to the jail in Virginia City.

Several of the buildings in Galena City had cellars. Mallory remembered hearing stories about how tunnels had connected some of the buildings back when the place was called Doldrums, so that a fella could disappear in one place and pop up in another across town without ever being seen. The Mormons who had founded the town had built the tunnels so that they could escape from the Gentile massacre they all feared. The massacre had never taken place, of course, and blasting at the mines in the surrounding hills had caused all those tunnels to collapse, but the cellars still remained. With their sturdy walls, hard-packed dirt floors, and no doors or windows, they were the closest thing Galena City had to a jail. This particular cellar was below the hardware store and the trapdoor opened into the store's back room.

The other outlaws started arguing over the hunks of bread and meat in the burlap sack. Mallory stepped forward and took it away from them, doling out the food as he saw fit. None of the others argued with his decisions, even though he kept the biggest share for himself.

While he was eating, somebody thumped on the trapdoor and called, "Hey, Mallory! You down there?"

That was the stagecoach driver, the one called George. He and the shotgunner had been taking turns standing guard over the prisoners. Mallory hated both of them already. He hated everybody in this stinking town. Especially that slut Nola and that rangy son of a bitch who had turned out to be a federal badge-toter . . .

"Yeah, I'm here," Mallory replied to George's question. "Where the hell else would I be?"

"Just thought you might be interested to know that somebody else stole all that silver."

"What!" Curses poured out of Mallory's mouth. "Who got it?" he finally managed to say, his snarling voice sounding more like an animal's than a man's.

"A woman named Nola Sutton, the one who owns that saloon up the street. Her and three of her girls drove off with a whole wagon full of silver earlier tonight."

"Nola? Nola did that?" Mallory threw back his head and screeched in rage and frustration. "The bitch! I'll kill her! She double-crosses me, then steals the silver herself . . . Aaarrghhh!"

162

The other prisoners crowded into the far side of the cellar, none of them wanting to get anywhere near Mallory at this moment.

"Don't worry, she won't get away with it," George called down through the heavy door. "Marshal Long's already gone after her, headed north toward the Truckee. I reckon he'll bring those women back, and the silver along with 'em. I surely hope so, anyway."

Mallory drew deep breaths into his body and tried to calm the storm of hate and fury raging inside him. Long and Nola had thwarted him at every turn, and now Nola had betrayed the lawman, too.

Mallory had to get out of here so that he could take his revenge on Nola, and on that big galoot of a lawdog, too. That was all there was to it.

He looked around the cellar, eyes burning feverishly, searching for some way out. The cellar was lit by a single candle sitting on the stump of a tree that had been cut down when the townsite was originally cleared. The feeble glow didn't reach into the corners, but Mallory had already explored them by feel and found nothing that could help him. Now he turned toward the stump itself, which was cracked and split with age. Mallory's lips were drawn back from his teeth in a grimace as he reached down and wrenched a long, thick piece of wood off the stump. He had thought of doing that earlier, when he was toying with the idea of using a chunk of broken wood as a makeshift shovel to dig his way out of the cellar.

That would take days, long days that he didn't have. He had to escape *now*.

One of the other outlaws came closer to him. The man's name was Zeb; he had his bullet-broken arm hanging in front of him in a crude sling. He said, "Ben, what are you doin' there—"

Mallory whipped around and lashed out with the broken piece of stump, raking it across Zeb's throat. The wood wasn't very sharp, but the jagged end was sharp enough to

163

rip through the soft flesh and tear veins. Blood gushed from Zeb's ruined throat as he gave a gurgling scream, staggered back, and collapsed. The blood looked black instead of red in the faint glow of the candle.

Only two of the other men were relatively able-bodied; the remaining outlaws had been wounded in the battles in which they had been captured. Mallory went for the two who were still on their feet, taking them by surprise. He rammed the makeshift stake into the throat of one man and grabbed the other one, strangling him and slamming his head against one of the thick beams supporting the building's floor, which formed the ceiling of the cellar. The other two men, one of whom was shot through the leg and the other who had been caught in the dynamite blast at the hideout cabin, started screaming in horror.

"Help!" bleated the man with the wounded leg as he tried to scramble away from Mallory and fell. "Mallory's gone crazy! He's gonna kill us all!"

Mallory was screaming, too, howling in insane rage. He drove the head of the man he was struggling with against the support beam until the outlaw's skull was grotesquely misshapen and his eyes had rolled up in his head. Mallory let go of the man and let him fall, then whirled around toward the others. The second man he had stabbed with the jagged piece of wood had managed to pull the crude weapon free, but that might have been a mistake, because it allowed the blood to flow that much faster from his throat. The front of his shirt was a gruesome mess as Mallory slammed into him and knocked him backward. The two wounded men screamed louder.

With all the yelling going on, Mallory didn't hear the bolts being pulled back on the trapdoor, but he knew it when strong arms grabbed him from behind. "Damn it, get away from those men!" yelled George.

Mallory drove an elbow backward into George's midsection, knocking the breath out of the guard. He twisted like an eel and got his hands on the rifle that George was carrying. George tried to pull it away, but Mallory's berserk strength was too much. Mallory twisted the rifle loose and brought it up sharply, cracking the butt against George's jaw. George went over backward, the knowledge of his own imminent death in his eyes.

Mallory shot him twice in the face, firing as quickly as he could pull the trigger and work the Winchester's lever.

He left the other two outlaws cringing in the cellar, not wanting to waste the bullets it would require to kill them.

Well, that plan, crude and impulsive though it had been, had worked out about as well as he could have hoped, thought Mallory as he kicked open the front door of the hardware store and raced out into the night. The store was closed at this hour, of course, as were most of the businesses in Galena City. Several horses were tied up at a hitch rack less than a block away, though. Mallory ran toward them.

The shots had been muffled by the thick walls of the cellar, but a few men were stepping out onto the boardwalks to investigate what they thought they had heard. One of them called to Mallory, "Hey! What are you—"

Mallory snapped a shot at the man, making him dive back into the building from which he had emerged.

Then Mallory was at the hitch rack, jerking loose the reins of the nearest horse and swinging up into its saddle. He slammed his heels into the horse's flanks and hauled its head around almost before he hit the leather. The horse lunged into a gallop.

Mallory raced out of Galena City, and as he rode, three thoughts filled his mind: Nola, that damned lawman . . . and all that silver. *His* silver . . .

# Chapter 19

Dawn found Longarm on the southern bank of the Truckee River. He had stopped there to rest his horse—and his own aching body—and to ponder the question of which way Nola, Angie, Rafaela, and Mickey might have gone from here.

To the north, across the river, was rugged, mostly unsettled country. That Paiute burial ground Mallory had been using as a hideout was up there, along with Virginia Peak and Pyramid Lake, but there wasn't much to attract four women, even four women on the run from the law.

To the west was Reno, a good-sized settlement. That was a definite possibility, thought Longarm. Reno was big enough so that four strangers wouldn't stand out too much, and Nola and her friends could catch a train there and head for San Francisco.

But trains ran east as well as west, and Longarm recalled that about fifteen miles east of his current location, the Truckee Valley also intersected the railroad, at a place called Two Mile Station. Longarm wasn't sure how the place had gotten its name, but it wasn't much of a settlement, little more than a flag stop depot, a water tank, a trading post, and a few cabins.

If Nola and her companions went there and caught an eastbound train, they would be beyond Longarm's reach in a matter of hours. In a few days, they could be in Chicago; a few days after that, New York or Lord only knew where else. The law would never find them, and that stolen silver would allow them to establish themselves in any kind of life they might choose.

For a lengthy moment, Longarm stood there on the bank of the river and thought about saying the hell with it. They hadn't really hurt anybody or anything—except his pride—and considering the lives they had led so far, maybe they deserved something better.

On the other hand, they didn't have any right to get that something better with somebody else's money, and if they used that stolen silver to finance their getaway, that was exactly what it would be. The law was still the law, after all.

"Damn," said Longarm. The word was quiet but heartfelt.

Then he swung up into his horse's saddle and turned the animal east, following the hunch his lawman's instincts had given him.

The old granny who was the closest thing Galena City had to a doctor had been roused from sleep and brought to the Silver Slipper to tend to his wounds. She had cleaned and rebandaged the bullet holes, then advised him, "Was I you, I'd go to bed for three or four days, sonny. You've bled too much here lately."

Longarm had shaken his head regretfully. "Afraid there's no time for that. I've got to get on the trail, or I won't catch up to the folks I'm after."

The old woman had just shaken her head. "It's your funeral, I reckon."

Longarm wasn't convinced that he was in that bad a shape, but he had to admit now as he rode alongside the river that he was mighty tired and even a little light-headed. He was confident he would be a match for the women when he caught up to them, though.

Unless he had gone in the wrong direction and never found them. He wasn't going to think about that . . .

Ben Mallory reined in when he reached the river. The sun was up now, making glints of light sparkle and dance on the swiftly flowing water. Before the winter was over, a sheet of ice might form over the river, but now, despite the cold air that made Mallory's breath fog in front of his face, the Truckee was still clear. Another man might have found the scenery to be downright beautiful.

Mallory paid no attention to anything except the hoofprints he spotted on the bank. Someone had ridden up here, paused, and then turned east, following the river upstream.

That damned star packer, thought Mallory. Had to be.

"I'm comin' to get you, lawman!" Mallory said with a cackle of laughter. He shook the stolen rifle over his head. "I'll kill you, you son of a bitch! Then I'll kill those damned whores!"

Viciously, he jabbed the heels of his boots into the flanks of his mount and started east, following the tracks left by Longarm's horse.

Longarm rode through the morning, gnawing on a stale biscuit he had stuck in the pocket of his coat before leaving Galena City and wishing he had a cup of hot coffee with a healthy slug of Maryland rye in it. That would go a long way toward making a fella feel human again, he knew. But he would have to wait until he got to a settlement again before he could have any coffee, let alone any laced with Tom Moore.

Now that the sun was up and shining brightly, he could see faint indications that a wagon had passed this way recently: crushed grass, overturned pebbles, even an occasional wheel track. Of course, there was no guarantee it was the right wagon, the one carrying Nola and the other women and the stolen silver, but Longarm's gut told him he was on their trail. He had no idea what the railroad schedule was or when the next eastbound train was due to roll in to Two Mile Station.

But Nola might know. She would have had plenty of time to check that out while he was recuperating from his injuries.

His mouth tightened grimly at that thought.

By mid-morning, he was riding into a huge, mostly barren sink ringed by mountain ranges that almost totally surrounded it. The river turned northward behind him, where the foothills ran out. The hard, rocky ground had a little downward slope to it, but not much, just enough so that he could see several miles to the east. That was why he could see the elevated water tank at Two Mile Station before he spotted any of the buildings themselves.

What made him lean forward in the saddle with interest, though, was the small dark shape moving rapidly in the same direction he was. Dust spiraled into the clear blue sky, kicked up by the wheels of the distant wagon and the hooves of the horses pulling it.

Longarm felt satisfaction but not any joy. The wagon was about halfway between him and Two Mile Station. He would catch up to it not long after it arrived at the flag stop.

That was when he saw something else from the corner of his eye that made him bite off a curse. Angling toward the settlement from the west, which meant it was off to his left as he rode northeast, was a tendril of smoke. The way it was moving, it had to be coming from the stack of a locomotive.

Nola had timed things close, all right. That was an eastbound train, and it would arrive in Two Mile Station right after the women drove up in the wagon.

According to Nola's plan, however, Longarm was still supposed to be back in Galena City, being freed right about now by the bartender for whom she had left a note the night before. She hadn't counted on him being less than a mile and a half behind them.

"Come on, horse," Longarm urged as he heeled the dun into a faster gait. "If you've got a run in you, now's the time to make it!"

The rangy animal leaped forward, stretching its legs as it broke into a gallop.

169

Longarm was so intent on what was ahead of him that he never looked back, never saw the rider emerging from the foothills and entering the sink hot on his trail.

That was Long up ahead, thought Mallory exultantly. For a moment, he considered reining in and getting off the stolen horse to try a long-distance shot with the rifle.

Then he discarded the idea. For one thing, that was too impersonal. He didn't want to kill the marshal from long range with a bullet that would slam into his back and knock him out of the saddle with no idea of where his fate had come from. Mallory wanted to see the terror in Long's eyes, wanted to witness the exquisite moment when life faded from those eyes forever.

Besides, it was too chancy, and for another thing, the lawman had just kicked his horse into a run. If Long was in a hurry, that could mean he was about to catch up to Nola and the other women. Mallory liked the idea of catching all of them together. Then he could make Long and Nola watch while he killed the other whores, before he moved on to them.

Mallory urged his own mount into a run. He had ridden the stolen horse hard all night and into the morning, but the animal would hold up a little while longer. Mallory was sure of it.

Nothing was going to prevent him from getting his revenge—and his silver.

Angie leaned forward and tapped Nola on the shoulder. She and Mickey were riding in the back of the wagon, while Nola and Rafaela were on the seat. Nola was handling the reins. She looked back and asked, "What is it?"

"Somebody on our back trail!" Angie said over the rumble of the iron-rimmed wheels on the hard ground.

Nola twisted her head more and stared back over the ground they had just covered. Less than a mile behind them, a rider was moving, the dark form fairly visible against the light-colored earth.

"Damn it, Custis!" exclaimed Nola. "Why couldn't you have stayed in Galena City?"

"How do you know that's Marshal Long following us?" asked Rafaela.

"Who else could it be? Who else is stubborn enough?"

"But how did he get loose so quick?" asked Angie, lifting a hand to shade her eyes as she tried to get a better look at their pursuer.

Nola shook her head and said, "I don't know. But after the past couple of weeks, I wouldn't put anything past that man." She slapped the reins against the backs of the horses pulling the wagon and shouted at them, urging them on to greater speed.

"We'll still get to Two Mile Station ahead of him," said Rafaela. "If the train isn't stopped for too long, it might pull out before he gets there."

"He can wire the next town," Nola said bitterly. "He can have the law waiting for us. Blast it, things weren't supposed to happen like this!"

"We can still get away," Angie said, a note of desperation edging into her voice. "Can't we?"

Abruptly, without any warning, Nola hauled on the reins and turned the horses due east. The sudden lurch made Angie and Mickey grab on to the sideboards of the wagon. "What are you doing?" screamed Rafaela, who had come close to being unseated by the move.

"We can't get away by boarding the train here," replied Nola as she prodded the team into a faster run. "We have to shake Custis off our trail first."

"But you're heading right into the middle of the sink!" protested Rafaela. "There's nothing out there—no settlements, no roads, nothing!"

"We can lose Custis and make it to Rock Creek," Nola insisted. "A spur line runs through there. We'll catch a train and be in Chicago before you know it!"

"Rock Creek is over a hundred miles away!"

"We can make it," said Nola. "We can make it!"

They weren't going to make it, Longarm thought. He had been surprised when the wagon turned away from Two Mile Station, but once he thought about it, he realized why Nola had made that decision. He was confident that it was Nola herself handling the reins; she wasn't the sort to turn the responsibility for their getaway over to any of the other women.

They must have spotted him, and Nola was trying to shake the pursuit before they boarded the train. The same thought had surely occurred to her that had come to him: even if they got away from him now, he could just wire ahead to the sheriff in Winnemucca and have the law waiting for them there.

What Nola ought to do was stop the wagon and surrender, Longarm told himself. She was heading now into some of the most desolate country on God's green earth. Only there was no green out there, just the brown and gray of sand and rock and mountains. He doubted very seriously if those women were prepared for the hardships that would face them on a trek through that barren wilderness. They would have to have a wagon full of food and water instead of silver if they were going to have any hope of making it alive.

Well, it wasn't going to come to that. He would catch up to them before they got very far. There was no way they could outrun him in the wagon. He had already closed the distance to a little under a mile, and the dun's long-legged, easy stride was closing the gap even more with every minute that passed.

Three-quarters of a mile . . . half a mile . . . less than a quarter of a mile separated them now. Longarm could see the women plainly. Their hats had come off, and their hair was streaming in the wind. He leaned forward in the saddle. When he rode alongside the wagon, he would try to catch the harness of one of the leaders and bring the team to a halt . . .

Smoke puffed from the back of the wagon, and he saw the faint flare of fire from the muzzle of a rifle, the flash washed out by the bright sunlight. They were shooting at him!

Angie worked the lever of the Winchester and blinked away the tears that welled up in her eyes. "I don't want to kill him!" she cried over the pounding of hooves.

"Just shoot over his head, I told you!" shouted Nola. "Scare him off!"

"Custis ain't going to scare off that easy," Angie muttered as she settled her cheek against the stock of the rifle and rested the butt of the weapon against her shoulder. She tilted the barrel skyward and pulled the trigger again.

The bullets weren't coming anywhere close to him, Longarm realized. The women were just trying to spook him and make him give up the chase. That wasn't going to happen.

They would have to kill him to stop him now.

Mallory was close enough that he could have risked a shot, but he was too caught up in the thrill of the chase. He had been surprised when the wagon turned away from the flag stop, but he recognized desperation when he saw it. He had felt it enough in himself when all the bastards in the world, the men with the money and power, conspired to keep him down, to deny him his due.

Sometimes desperation worked. Driven by it, he had reached out and seized power for himself, and along with it a fortune in silver. He had only been taking what was rightfully his, though.

The fear he had inspired in the mine superintendents, the sons of bitches who had made life so miserable for him, was just a sweet bonus.

Mallory kept riding, drawing ever closer to those he was pursuing.

They would have gotten away if not for bad luck. That was the thought that flashed through Nola's mind as the wagon lurched over a large rock she hadn't seen until it was too late, and a sharp cracking sound came to her ears.

The front axle had snapped.

An instant later, the right front corner of the wagon dipped violently as the wheel on that side came spinning off. Rafaela, Angie, and Mickey all screamed. Nola's mouth was clamped tightly shut as she sawed at the reins and tried to pull off a miracle through sheer force of will.

The wagon tipped and went over in a grinding, rolling crash.

Nola felt herself flying through the air for a second that seemed much longer than it actually was, then she slammed into the hard ground with breathtaking force. She had forced her body to go limp, so her momentum sent her rolling over and over in a loose sprawl. She came to a stop on her belly. She was more numb than hurting. With a shake of her head to try to clear away some of the cobwebs from her stunned brain, she pushed herself up and looked around for the other women.

The wagon was smashed almost to kindling, but the heavy bags of silver still lay amidst the rubble. The horses had broken loose, snapping their harness, and were galloping away seemingly unhurt. Nola spotted Mickey lying motionless, not far from the wagon, her long black hair spread out like a fan around her head. She couldn't see Rafaela or Angie.

Nola lurched to her feet and staggered a couple of steps to the side as the rattle of hoofbeats made her turn her head. Longarm galloped up to the wreckage, his face grim as he brought his horse to a skidding halt. He was out of the saddle in the blink of an eye and hurrying toward her.

"Nola!" he called. "Are you all right?"

She didn't say anything, but she knew she would never be all right again.

Longarm caught hold of her arms. She was so shaken she didn't even think to check and see if the pistol was still in its holster on her hip. Anyway, she couldn't fight him now. It was all over. Her plan was ruined, and even worse than that, she had been responsible for the deaths of her three friends . . .

Mickey groaned and sat up, shaking her head. Nola felt relief throb through her. At least one of them wasn't dead. She looked up into the face of the big lawman who held her and said raggedly, "R-Rafaela? Angie?"

"I saw 'em on the other side of the wagon as I rode up," said Longarm. "They were thrown clear just like you and Mickey. Didn't look like they were hurt too bad. Leastways, they were both moving around."

Nola closed her eyes for a second. They were all alive. Her plan had failed, but at least she hadn't killed anybody—

More hoofbeats made her eyes snap open, and she looked past Longarm to see the man racing toward them on horseback. He threw a rifle to his shoulder and started blazing away as he guided the horse with his knees.

*Mallory!*

Longarm was already twisting and reaching for his gun as Mallory swept in on them, screaming insanely, "I'll kill you all! Gimme my silver!" Longarm was already off balance and didn't expect the hard shove that Nola suddenly gave him. He fell.

Even as he was falling, he heard the ugly thud of a bullet striking flesh and the grunt of pain that came from Nola. Longarm rolled and came up on one knee, letting instinct control his muscles as he palmed out his Colt from the cross-draw rig and lifted it. Mallory was suddenly there in front of him, filling his vision, and he pulled the trigger smoothly, once, twice, three times. The Colt bucked against his palm as the shots rolled out like thunder. Mallory screeched as the slugs drove into his body and lifted him out of the saddle.

175

Arms outflung, he landed on his back. Blood bubbled from the holes in his chest.

Longarm got to his feet. Only his iron nerves kept him from shaking a little, but he was able to hold the gun rock-steady as he walked over to Mallory. The outlaw was staring sightlessly up into the sun, but he was still alive. His lips were moving.

"M-my silver . . ." he rasped.

"Spend it in hell, you son of a bitch," said Longarm. The words blended with the macabre rattle that came from Mallory's throat. One final shudder and he was dead.

Longarm swung away from the corpse and went hurriedly to Nola. She had fallen on her side, and when Longarm gently rolled her onto her back, he saw the blood on her shirt. She was pale and her features were drawn with pain, but she was conscious. "C-Custis . . . ?" she said.

"Right here with you," Longarm told her. He figured she had a minute, maybe less. When she lifted one hand a little, he caught it tightly in his.

"Can't blame . . . a gal for trying," she whispered. "Lord, I wish I'd met you . . . a long time ago . . ."

"Me, too," said Longarm.

"Mallory?"

"He's dead."

"Good," she breathed. She looked up at Longarm and somehow smiled. "The other girls . . . don't . . . don't . . . ah!"

She was gone. Gently, Longarm closed her eyes for her. Gone before she could extract from him the promise she had been trying to get.

But he knew what she wanted.

The question now was whether or not he could give it to her.

# Chapter 20

"He wants to see you," said Henry, a hint of smug satisfaction in his voice as he glanced over his shoulder toward the door of the chief marshal's office.

Longarm nodded, an unlit cheroot clenched between his teeth. "Reckon I'd better go right in, then."

"Yes, I'd say so. In fact, Marshal Vail was expecting you before now. I told him I'd send you in to see him as soon as you showed up."

Longarm tried not to grin. Henry sounded pleased with himself. Over the years, he and Longarm had come to a sort of understanding so that they didn't despise each other, but Henry still liked the idea that Longarm was going to get his ass chewed on by Billy Vail.

Of course, Henry was wrong if he thought Longarm cared about what was going to happen. Right now, Longarm just didn't give a damn.

He opened the door without knocking, stalked into Vail's office, and settled himself in the red leather chair in front of the desk. Vail looked up from the papers spread out in front of him, raised his eyebrows, and said bitingly, "Well, make yourself comfortable."

"Thanks, Billy," said Longarm. "I intend to."

Vail shoved the papers aside. "I'll get right to the point.

How the *hell* did you manage to let those other three women escape?''

Longarm didn't answer for a moment. He filled the time instead by taking out a lucifer and scratching it to life on the sole of his left boot. He left his ankle cocked on his other knee as he lit the cheroot and blew a puff of smoke in the general direction of the banjo clock on the wall.

Then he pointed the cheroot at the papers and said mildly, ''It's all in my report, Billy.''

Vail controlled his temper with a visible effort. ''I want you to tell me.''

Longarm shrugged. ''All right, but it's a waste of time. The ladies were so shaken up by being tossed out of that wagon when it crashed that I didn't think I could make them walk back to Two Mile Station. The wagon team had run off already, or I would've caught them and let the women ride to the settlement. So there was really nothing I could do except leave them there while I went to get a wagon so I could haul them and that stolen silver in.''

''But when you got back from Two Mile Station, they were gone!''

Longarm nodded and said solemnly, ''I reckon I made an error in judgment, Billy. I sure didn't think they were up to walking away from there like that.''

''And you decided not to go after them because . . . ?''

''I didn't think I ought to just leave all that silver there. Figured I ought to get it safe under lock and key first.''

Vail brought a clenched fist down hard on the desk. ''Only it wasn't all there when you got back, was it? Three of the ingots were gone!''

Longarm shook his head. ''I sure was disappointed in those women. They promised me they'd stay right there until I came back for them.''

Vail sat back in his chair and blew out a gusty breath. ''You're not fooling me for a second, Custis,'' he said. ''You can write a report that makes you look like a damned fool, but I know you aren't one. And I'm not one, either.''

"Never said you were, Billy. You're a mighty smart man. Smart enough to know that sometimes no matter what a fella does, he finds himself stuck between a rock and a hard place."

"Well, this isn't the first time you've been there, is it?" grumped Vail. He gathered up the papers, straightened them roughly, pulled open a drawer and threw them inside. "All right, get out of here. I have to think. I'm going to come up with the worst damn job I possibly can, and then I'm going to dump it right in your lap. It's liable to take me a while, but I'll come up with something."

"Whatever you say, Billy." Longarm stood up and left the office.

Henry was waiting, a faint look of disappointment on his face. "I didn't hear any real shouting," he said.

Longarm grinned and threw the pasty-faced clerk a bone. "Sometimes it's worse that way," he said.

A cold wind was blowing down Colfax Avenue as Longarm paused on the steps of the federal building to pull his coat a little tighter around him and tug his hat down. He was looking forward to finding a warm saloon and a warmer woman.

That thought brought back memories that made him grimace slightly. He wasn't sure he would ever forget Nola Sutton. He would have rather remembered her the way she was when she was alive, but the way she had looked when he loaded her body in the back of the wagon he'd brought from Two Mile Station was etched into his brain. He had put Mallory's body in the back of the wagon, too, along with the silver—except for the one ingot apiece that Angie, Rafaela, and Mickey had taken with them when he'd let them go. Maybe that was enough for a new start for them and maybe it wasn't, but it was all he had been able to bring himself to do. He just hoped they had been able to flag down a train after they'd trudged the several miles north to the Central Pacific rails.

On the way back to Galena City with the bodies and the

silver in the borrowed wagon, Longarm had run into a posse led by Charlie Dodson and that young shotgun guard Pryor. They had started after him when Pryor discovered that Mallory had killed George and escaped. Longarm was sorry to hear about the stagecoach driver. George had been a good man.

That had wrapped everything up, and in due course, Longarm had come back here to Denver, where he planned to spend at least a couple of weeks resting and recovering from the bullet wound in his side. It still ached a little, especially on cold days like this one. Longarm went down the steps of the federal building and turned to walk along Colfax Avenue.

He had gone less than a block when someone behind him said, "Custis?"

Longarm turned, saw the woman standing there in a bonnet and coat and long dress. Her face had been scrubbed clean of the saloon girl's war paint, and her blond hair was plaited into two heavy braids that hung down on her shoulders. She looked like she was fresh off the farm, instead of going back there, which was what Longarm devoutly hoped she was going to do.

"Angie," he said quietly. "You shouldn't be here."

"I just had to see you again," she said as she stepped closer to him. "I'm going home."

Longarm nodded. "I'm glad to hear it."

He wished Amelia Loftus had turned around and gone home while she still had the chance. Some folks just weren't lucky enough to ever have that opportunity. From what Nola had said, home to her had been nothing but a living hell, and the same was probably true of Mickey. He had never heard Rafaela's story, he realized. Probably never would.

As for him, it had been too many years, too many miles, since a gawky, long-legged country boy had left West-by-God Virginia. For better or worse, this was his home now.

Angie laid a hand on his arm. "I'd like to give you a proper farewell, Custis." Despite her appearance, at that moment she was a saloon girl again, lust shining in her eyes.

"Some place with clean sheets and a soft mattress."

Longarm shook his head and said, "You best get out of that habit, Angie. Go marry some young fella who's got a nice piece of land and raise a whole passel of youngsters. If I was you, I'd just forget about everything that's happened since you came west."

Her hand tightened on his arm. "How can I just forget everything like that?"

Longarm wasn't sure what to tell her. He said, "That's a damned good question. I wish I knew."

Watch for

**LONGARM AND THE KANSAS JAILBIRD**

243rd novel in the exciting LONGARM series
from Jove

*Coming in March!*

# LONGARM

Explore the exciting Old West with
one of the men who made it wild!

_LONGARM AND THE DURANGO DOUBLE-CROSS
    #231                           0-515-12244-0/$4.99
_LONGARM AND THE WHISKEY CREEK
    WIDOW #232                  0-515-12265-3/$4.99
_LONGARM AND THE BRANDED BEAUTY
    #233                           0-515-12278-5/$4.99
_LONGARM AND THE RENEGADE ASSASSINS
    #234                           0-515-12292-0/$4.99
_LONGARM AND THE WICKED
    SCHOOLMARM #235           0-515-12302-1/$4.99
_LONGARM AND THE RIVER PIRATES #236  0-515-12340-4/$4.99
_LONGARM AND THE HATCHET WOMAN #237  0-515-12356-0/$4.99
_LONGARM AND THE BLOSSOM ROCK BANSHEE
    #238                           0-515-12372-2/$4.99
_LONGARM AND THE GRAVE ROBBERS #239  0-515-12392-7/$4.99
_LONGARM AND THE NEVADA NYMPHS #240  0-515-12411-7/$4.99
_LONGARM AND THE COLORADO COUNTERFEITER
    #241                           0-515-12437-0/$4.99
_LONGARM GIANT #18: LONGARM AND THE DANISH
    DAMES                        0-515-12435-4/$5.50
_LONGARM AND THE RED-LIGHT LADIES #242  0-515-12450-8/$4.99
_LONGARM AND THE KANSAS JAILBIRD#243 (3/99)  0-515-12468-0/$4.99

Payable in U.S. funds only. No cash/COD accepted. Postage & handling: U.S./CAN. $2.75 for one
book, $1.00 for each additional, not to exceed $6.75; Int'l $5.00 for one book, $1.00 each additional.
We accept Visa, Amex, MC ($10.00 min.), checks ($15.00 fee for returned checks) and money
orders. Call 800-788-6262 or 201-933-9292, fax 201-896-8569; refer to ad #201g

| Penguin Putnam Inc. | Bill my: ☐Visa ☐MasterCard ☐Amex _____ (expires) |
|---|---|
| P.O. Box 12289, Dept. B | Card#_____ |
| Newark, NJ 07101-5289 | Signature_____ |

Please allow 4-6 weeks for delivery.
Foreign and Canadian delivery 6-8 weeks.

## Bill to:

Name_____

Address_____City_____

State/ZIP_____

Daytime Phone #_____

## Ship to:

| Name_____ | Book Total | $_____ |
|---|---|---|
| Address_____ | Applicable Sales Tax | $_____ |
| City_____ | Postage & Handling | $_____ |
| State/ZIP_____ | Total Amount Due | $_____ |

**This offer subject to change without notice.**

# JAKE LOGAN

## TODAY'S HOTTEST ACTION WESTERN!

___SLOCUM #224: LOUISIANA LOVELY                    0-515-12176-2/$4.99
___SLOCUM #225: PRAIRIE FIRES                       0-515-12190-8/$4.99
___SLOCUM AND THE REAL McCOY #226                   0-515-12208-4/$4.99
___SLOCUM #227: BLOOD ON THE BRAZOS                 0-515-12229-7/$4.99
___SLOCUM AND THE SCALPLOCK TRAIL #228              0-515-12243-2/$4.99
___SLOCUM AND THE TEXAS ROSE #229                   0-515-12264-5/$4.99
___SLOCUM AND THE COMELY CORPSE #230                0-515-12277-7/$4.99
___SLOCUM #231: BLOOD IN KANSAS                     0-515-12291-2/$4.99
___SLOCUM AND THE GREAT DIAMOND
                        HOAX #232                   0-515-12301-3/$4.99
___SLOCUM AND THE LONE STAR FEUD #233               0-515-12339-0/$4.99
___SLOCUM AND THE LAST GASP #234                    0-515-12355-2/$4.99
___SLOCUM AND THE MINER'S JUSTICE #235              0-515-12371-4/$4.99
___SLOCUM AT HELL'S ACRE #236                       0-515-12391-9/$4.99
___SLOCUM AND THE WOLF HUNT #237                    0-515-12413-3/$4.99
___SLOCUM AND THE BARONESS #238                     0-515-12436-2/$4.99
___SLOCUM AND THE COMANCHE PRINCESS #239
                                                    0-51512449-4/$4.99
___SLOCUM AND THE LIVE OAK BOYS #240 (3/99)         0-515-12467-2/$4.99

Payable in U.S. funds only. No cash/COD accepted. Postage & handling: U.S./CAN. $2.75 for one
book, $1.00 for each additional, not to exceed $6.75; Int'l $5.00 for one book, $1.00 each additional.
We accept Visa, Amex, MC ($10.00 min.), checks ($15.00 fee for returned checks) and money
orders. Call 800-788-6262 or 201-933-9292, fax 201-896-8569; refer to ad #202d

Penguin Putnam Inc.          Bill my: ☐Visa ☐MasterCard ☐Amex_____ (expires)
P.O. Box 12289, Dept. B      Card#_____
Newark, NJ 07101-5289        Signature_____
Please allow 4-6 weeks for delivery.
Foreign and Canadian delivery 6-8 weeks.

**Bill to:**

Name_____

Address_____ City_____

State/ZIP_____

Daytime Phone #_____

**Ship to:**

Name_____ Book Total          $_____

Address_____ Applicable Sales Tax $_____

City_____ Postage & Handling  $_____

State/ZIP_____ Total Amount Due    $_____

This offer subject to change without notice.

# J. R. ROBERTS
# THE
# GUNSMITH

| | | |
|---|---|---|
| THE GUNSMITH #190: | LADY ON THE RUN | 0-515-12163-0/$4.99 |
| THE GUNSMITH #191: | OUTBREAK | 0-515-12179-7/$4.99 |
| THE GUNSMITH #192: | MONEY TOWN | 0-515-12192-4/$4.99 |
| GUNSMITH GIANT #3: | SHOWDOWN AT | |
| | LITTLE MISERY | 0-515-12210-6/$5.99 |
| THE GUNSMITH #193: | TEXAS WIND | 0-515-12231-9/$4.99 |
| THE GUNSMITH #194: | MASSACRE AT ROCK | |
| | SPRINGS | 0-515-12245-9/$4.99 |
| THE GUNSMITH #195: | CRIMINAL KIN | 0-515-12266-1/$4.99 |
| THE GUNSMITH #196: | THE COUNTERFEIT | |
| | CLERGYMAN | 0-515-12279-3/$4.99 |
| THE GUNSMITH #197: | APACHE RAID | 0-515-12293-9/$4.99 |
| THE GUNSMITH #198: | THE LADY KILLERS | 0-515-12303-X/$4.99 |
| THE GUNSMITH #199: | DENVER DESPERADOES | 0-515-12341-2/$4.99 |
| THE GUNSMITH #200: | THE JAMES BOYS | 0-515-12357-9/$4.99 |
| THE GUNSMITH #201: | THE GAMBLER | 0-515-12373-0/$4.99 |
| THE GUNSMITH #202: | VIGILANTE JUSTICE | 0-515-12393-5/$4.99 |
| THE GUNSMITH #203: | DEAD MAN'S BLUFF | 0-515-12414-1/$4.99 |
| THE GUNSMITH #204: | WOMEN ON THE RUN | 0-515-12438-9/$4.99 |
| THE GUNSMITH #205: | THE GAMBLER'S GIRL | 0-515-12451-6/$4.99 |
| THE GUNSMITH #206: | LEGEND OF THE | |
| | PIASA BIRD (3/99) | 0-515-12469-9/$4.99 |

Prices slightly higher in Canada

Payable in U.S. funds only. No cash/COD accepted. Postage & handling: U.S./CAN. $2.75 for one book, $1.00 for each additional, not to exceed $6.75; Int'l $5.00 for one book, $1.00 each additional. We accept Visa, Amex, MC ($10.00 min.), checks ($15.00 fee for returned checks) and money orders.  Call 800-788-6262 or 201-933-9292, fax 201-896-8569; refer to ad #206g

| | |
|---|---|
| **Penguin Putnam Inc.** | Bill my: ☐Visa ☐MasterCard ☐Amex _____ (expires) |
| **P.O. Box 12289, Dept. B** | Card#_____ |
| **Newark, NJ 07101-5289** | Signature_____ |
| Please allow 4-6 weeks for delivery. | |
| Foreign and Canadian delivery 6-8 weeks. | |

## Bill to:

Name_____

Address_____City_____

State/ZIP_____

Daytime Phone #_____

## Ship to:

| | | |
|---|---|---|
| Name_____ | Book Total | $_____ |
| Address_____ | Applicable Sales Tax | $_____ |
| City_____ | Postage & Handling | $_____ |
| State/ZIP_____ | Total Amount Due | $_____ |

**This offer subject to change without notice.**

# From the creators of Longarm!
# BUSHWHACKERS

They were the most brutal gang of cutthroats ever assembled. And during the Civil War, they sought justice outside of the law—paying back every Yankee raid with one of their own. They rode hard, shot straight, and had their way with every willin' woman west of the Mississippi. No man could stop them. No woman could resist them. And no Yankee stood a chance of living when Quantrill's Raiders rode into town...

Win and Joe Coulter become the two most wanted men in the West. And they learn just how sweet—and deadly—revenge could be...

---

**BUSHWHACKERS by B. J. Lanagan**
0-515-12102-9/$4.99
**BUSHWHACKERS #2: REBEL COUNTY**
0-515-12142-8/$4.99
**BUSHWHACKERS#3:**
**THE KILLING EDGE** 0-515-12177-0/$4.99
**BUSHWHACKERS #4:**
**THE DYING TOWN** 0-515-12232-7/$4.99
**BUSHWHACKERS #5:**
**MEXICAN STANDOFF** 0-515-12263-7/$4.99
**BUSHWHACKERS #6:**
**EPITAPH** 0-515-12290-4/$4.99

---

Prices slightly higher in Canada

Payable in U.S. funds only. No cash/COD accepted. Postage & handling: U.S./CAN. $2.75 for one book, $1.00 for each additional, not to exceed $6.75; Int'l $5.00 for one book, $1.00 each additional. We accept Visa, Amex, MC ($10.00 min.), checks ($15.00 fee for returned checks) and money orders. Call 800-788-6262 or 201-933-9292, fax 201-896-8569; refer to ad # 705

| Penguin Putnam Inc. | Bill my: ☐Visa ☐MasterCard ☐Amex _____ (expires) |
|---|---|
| P.O. Box 12289, Dept. B | Card# _____ |
| Newark, NJ 07101-5289 | |
| Please allow 4-6 weeks for delivery. | Signature _____ |

Foreign and Canadian delivery 6-8 weeks.

**Bill to:**
Name _____
Address _____ City _____
State/ZIP _____
Daytime Phone # _____

**Ship to:**
Name _____ Book Total $ _____
Address _____ Applicable Sales Tax $ _____
City _____ Postage & Handling $ _____
State/ZIP _____ Total Amount Due $ _____

This offer subject to change without notice.